Rebellion Brewing?

Torm snorted. "Co-operation! The Earth doesn't want co-operation, the Earth wants slaves! We've dealt squarely with Earth, and they've cheated us and betrayed us and degraded us—"

"And I suppose that these smuggled supplies are part of your policy of dealing squarely with Earth?"

Torm's face was white. "I tell you in all truth that we've received nothing in this colony that we don't need—*for survival.* You aren't dealing with the same conditions here as on Earth. The men need more food than the average Earthman. And there are contamination problems—"

The Colonel's eyes were dark. "And I suppose your people eat metal, Mr. Torm. I suppose they eat *tool steel?*"

Then, quite suddenly, the men heard an unearthly screech. . . .

To JOE

For his help along the way

Oh, East is East, and West is West, and never
    the twain shall meet,
Till Earth and Sky stand presently at God's
    great Judgment Seat;
But their is neither East nor West, Border,
    nor Breed, nor Birth
When two strong men stand face to face, though
    they come from the ends of the earth!

—RUDYARD KIPLING

From: "The Ballad of East and West" from DEPARTMENTAL DITTIES AND BALLADS AND BARRACK-ROOM BALLADS, by Rudyard Kipling, reprinted by permission of Mrs. George Bambridge and Doubleday & Company, Inc., and Messrs. Methuen & Co., Ltd., and The Macmillan Company of Canada.

TROUBLE ON TITAN

ALAN E. NOURSE

LANCER BOOKS • NEW YORK

A LANCER BOOK • 1967

TROUBLE ON TITAN

LANCER BOOKS, INC. • 185 MADISON AVENUE • NEW YORK, N.Y. 10016

Introduction:

I'VE NEVER BEEN THERE

Oₙₑ ᴏғ ᴛʜᴇ ᴍᴏꜱᴛ exciting things about science fiction, both reading it and writing it, is the freedom of imagination it offers to both the reader and the writer.

It's perfectly true that adventure stories, and Indian stories, and mystery stories, and stories of history and exploration are imaginative. I'd be the last to deny it. But they all have strings attached. We know a great deal about the Indians, for instance—historical facts, figures, geographical data, biographies. We can't make Sitting Bull a Navaho. We can't write a story about the Indians that violates any of the known facts about them, and if we read a story that does, we toss the book aside and say, "that fellow isn't much of a writer—" But in science fiction, neither the writer nor the reader has any such narrow limitations.

Perhaps I'd better modify that just a little, before the tried-and-true science fiction readers start crawling down my throat. There *are* limitations in science fiction which the readers demand, and which the writers must obey. But the limitations are different in science fiction—and it's that difference that makes these stories so exciting to me.

I think Tʀᴏᴜʙʟᴇ ᴏɴ Tɪᴛᴀɴ is a good story to illustrate my point. Basically, this is a free-wheeling adventure story. But in writing it, I could not violate what is already proved, known fact about the background where the story is set, or the events in the course of the story. If my book had been set in San Francisco during the great earthquake, I'd have been very limited in the picture I could have painted with the story. But it *wasn't* set in San Francisco. It was set on Titan, the fifth moon of Saturn—and here, my friends, we can take off with a vengeance. Because I've never been on Titan—*and neither has anybody else!*

In planning the story, I had to ask myself, "What do we really know about Titan?" A surprising amount, for a place we've never come close to approaching. We know, for instance, that it *is* a moon, circling the sixth planet of our Solar System much the same as our Moon circles the Earth. We   ow that it has at least eight brother and sister moons circling the same planet: Mimas, Enceladus, Tethys, Dione, Rhea, Hyperion, Japetus, and Phoebe. We even know that it *might* have another— Themis, which was reported by Professor Pickering in 1905, and has not been seen since. But of all these moons, we know that Titan is the largest, approximately 3,550 miles in diameter (compared to our own Moon's 2,160 miles in diameter). We know that Titan makes one complete revolution around Saturn in a period of 15.94 days, that its mean distance from its planet is 759,000 miles, and that of all the moons of Saturn, Titan is the only one that has an atmosphere.

Well, that still gave me room enough to move around quite a bit. What kind of atmosphere could we look for on Titan? By use of the spectrograph, astronomers have determined that it contains large amounts of methane. Astronomers suspect ammonia, too, as well as cyanogen and water vapor. In short, a thoroughly poisonous atmosphere very similar to, but less dense than, that of Saturn herself. Further, since the structure of Saturn, like Jupiter and Uranus, is probably a huge core of rock and mineral material surrounded by a thick ice pack and an outer blanket of volatile material, it's safe to assume that Titan would be a rather large and bitterly cold chunk of rock and metal.

6

You can see upon examination of these facts that we still aren't hemmed in very much. We can have fun speculating on some of the possibilities of a planetoid with a methane atmosphere. Mines, under the surface, would require either positive pressure oxygen to enable the miners to work, or else they would have to work constantly in protective suits—a clumsy arrangement, as you know if you've ever hopped into a diver's suit. But with oxygen in the tunnel, and methane on the surface—leaks would spell trouble. Still, the same principle of methane burning in oxygen would be very useful if one wanted to do some welding out on the surface—or if one wanted to pilot a small jet plane, for that matter.

There were other limitations, too. One of them was quite basic to the story, and is basic to thinking about space travel and eventual travel to other star systems. It's a point that many science fiction writers either ignore altogether or sideswipe in a most disgraceful fashion. Taking a rocket ship to the Moon, or to Mars, or to Venus, or to Titan is one thing. Taking a rocket to another star system is quite different. The distance is prohibitive, unless a ship could somehow accelerate enough to cut the time of the star-journey down to something reasonable. But a fine old gentleman named Einstein has put the lid on that for us. The speed of light is approximately 186,000 miles per second. Thou shalt go no faster. Thou shalt not even approach that speed without having upsetting things happen—unless the current theories of the nature of space and time are way off base. And we have no right to assume that they are without a great deal of justification.

Well, to a culture which has gone to the planets, and is looking for new worlds to conquer, an interstellar drive of *any* sort would be quite a plum. Yet we know of one interstellar drive that exists right now—!

TROUBLE ON TITAN is a free-wheeling adventure story. It makes no claim to be anything else. But if the story of

7

Tuck Benedict and David Torm makes you pause and think a bit, perhaps even to reshape your ideas about the people in the world about you just a trifle, it was worth the writing a thousand times over. I hope you enjoy reading it as much as I enjoyed writing it!

A.E.N.

Contents

Chapter 1

THE MISSION

"TELEGRAM! Telegram for Tucker Benedict!" Tuck Benedict awoke with a start, jarred from his troubled, fuzzy dream. At first he couldn't orient himself; then he recognized the curved glass windows and the corridor of the giant cross-country jet liner. The trim, blue-uniformed figure of the stewardess was moving down the aisle, and he caught her eye as she passed his seat.

"I'm Tucker Benedict," he said.

The stewardess smiled, and handed him the folded blue envelope. "This came in just after we left Denver," she said. "Hope it's good news!"

Tuck nodded and took the envelope, pulling the little plastic opener-tab with trembling fingers. In these days of fast rocket mail, a telegram was an event. Who could be wiring him? Certainly not someone back at school. He was a graduate now, his diploma was carefully placed away in its folder in his inside jacket pocket, and with it the letter that was far more precious to him than any diploma in the world: the letter from the Dean of Admissions of the Polytechnic Institute of Earth, announcing that he had been accepted at the Institute with the next incoming class. Even as he thought of it, Tuck's heart skipped a beat, and a chill of apprehension shivered up his spine. Could something have gone wrong with the minds now, not with the formal announcements to be scholarship? They *couldn't* have changed their minds made at the International Rocketry Exhibit in just two days— The blue tissue of the telegram crackled in his hand as he laid it open, and he hardly dared to breathe as he read it:

PERSON TO PERSON TUCKER BENEDICT
CARE OF INTERNATIONAL JET FLIERS INC.
EN ROUTE NEW YORK:
DEAR TUCK ARRIVED CATSKILL ROCKET PORT THIS
MORNING WILL MEET YOUR JET IN NEW YORK
CAN YOU MISS A DAY OF THE EXHIBIT? MARS
JOB CLEANED UP HOME FOR A SANDWICH
AT LEAST LOVE DAD

Tuck sat back in the deep jet-liner seat, undecided whether to laugh or cry or whoop for joy. Dad was home! After three long, long years, dad was home again, waiting to meet him in New York! He sat staring through the plexiglass window, looking down on the green and white and silvery pattern passing on the ground far below, hardly able to believe the wonderful news. He remembered clearly the note his father had sent him from Mars at Christmas time—and at that time Colonel Benedict had not expected to be home for another two years at least. But now—in his excitement Tuck could hardly sit still. In just another half-hour he would be seeing his father!

Tuck and his father had been very close, not so many years before. Tuck had been too young to remember when his mother died, and his earliest recollections were of life with dad in the big, spacious New York apartment, high above the Hudson River overlooking the beautiful terraced parks and smoothly winding highways of the great metropolis. Those had been happy years, before his father had been persuaded to join the Security Commission, the "Interplanetary Trouble Shooters," as the Colonel called it, to be sent from one end of the Solar System to the other on jobs of investigation and diplomacy. The Colonel had been with the Commission for over eight years, and Tuck was justifiably proud that his father had risen to a position of importance—after all, the Security Commission was one of the most critical cogs in the whole great commercial machine that had spread out from the cities of Earth to all corners of the Solar System. But Tuck was jealous of the times when his father was away, perhaps tracing down missing supplies that had never reached their destination at the colony on Mars, perhaps smoothing out the bitter feelings of the groups working on the rehabilitation of Venus, perhaps persuading the miners far out in the Asteroid Rings to obey the channeling and landing procedures when they came back home to weigh in their precious cargoes of platinum and uranium. These trips had been long, sometimes taking Colonel Benedict away for years, and busy as Tuck was with his studies, he had always dreamed of the time when dad would come home for good, and the two of them could take up the old life where they had left it.

Tuck frowned, his steady gray eyes scanning the telegram again, a puzzled frown crossing his forehead. "Home for a sandwich at least," his father had said. Could that mean that this was to be only a short stay, another of those brief visits back to Earth after a long assignment? There was something odd about the tone of the telegram—it didn't sound quite like dad. But they could worry about that together when the liner reached New York. It was enough for now that he was to see his father again, after all these long years.

Happily, Tuck stared through the observation bay that opened almost to the door alongside his feet. He was a sturdy-looking youth, rather slight of build, but wiry, and browned from the West Coast sun. His gray eyes were lively in a grave, thoughtful face, and his short brown hair had succumbed to a neat combing, perhaps for the first time in months, and only after long and diligent persuasion. As the jet motors hummed in his ears, he was far too excited to sleep again, and the minutes passed slowly. Far, far below, through the blanket of hazy white clouds, he caught a glimpse of the long, straight double ribbons of silver crossing the broad plains, the New York-Los Angeles Rolling Roads that carried the huge volumes of overland freight across the continent. Far to the north the Rocky Mountains were giving way to rolling plains, and by squinting a good deal and watching closely he could just make out the great glowing dome of the Montana Solar Energy Converter. He had visited this great plant once, during the years at Prep, and he knew several of his classmates who had been accepted at the Solar Energy School in Helena, to study the theory and engineering behind Solar Energy Conversion. The great plants all over the world converted the enormous energy of the sunlight into heat, light and power to supply the luxurious cities and quiet suburban towns, and the ruthenium from the lonely outpost mining colony on Titan was the catalyst which made this energy conversion possible.

Yet for all its importance and complexity, Tuck could never have become interested in Solar Energy work as a career. For him there was only one field, only one work of importance, and he itched with impatience to get started, to begin the studies that would lead him to his goal.

It was not that there was anything so wonderful and new about rocket travel. The first rocket from Earth reached the moon well over two hundred years before, in 1976. In A.D. 2180, the year that Tuck was born, the rocket ship *Planet Nine* had returned from Pluto, the farthest planet from the sun, with a complete file of maps, surface data, exploratory notes, and astronomical data on Pluto, as well as astro-photographs of the tenth planet that had been discovered skimming its frigid course still farther out in the blackness of space. A large farming colony had been thriving on Mars for a hundred and fifty years, and the great Solar Converter being built on Venus would soon be at work reconverting those arid deserts and windswept crags into a lush tropical paradise for farmers and vacationers. The exploration of the Solar System was almost complete, except for the mopping up—but there were other frontiers, greater frontiers, and

14

these were the frontiers that excited Tuck. For beyond the limits of the Solar System lay the black wastes of deep space, the unbridgeable gulf that led to the stars. And someday, Tuck knew, some man would find a way to go to the stars—

Tuck sat back in his seat, fingering the letter of acceptance to the Polytechnic Institute excitedly. Some man would learn a way, some man would discover how to take a rocket ship and leave the Solar System light-years behind, and go to the stars. And all his life Tuck had dreamed that he might be that man—

The liner landed just at dusk. From the bay Tuck strained his eyes trying to see his father's familiar figure, waiting in the crowd behind the blast barrier, but the bright lights threw the people into darkness. Carefully he checked his bags with the automatic redcap, punching the address of his father's apartment on the metal consignment tape; then he gathered up his coat and followed the crowd down the gangway onto the smooth concrete of the landing platform, still trying to peer ahead into the darkness. And then he saw Colonel Benedict, standing tall and straight, his gray hair crisp, blue eyes wrinkled into a quizzical smile. Tuck let out a cry, and broke into a run, working his way through the crowd, and then he was wringing his father's hand, and the two of them were trying to talk at once as they made their way down into the Terminal Building.

"But you said in your last letter that it might be two more years—I had no idea that you'd be back so soon—"

The Colonel's eyes twinkled. "I just wanted to see if you could still take a surprise."

"Surprise! I almost dropped through the seat!" Tuck regarded his father proudly. "Dad, it's wonderful. You couldn't look better."

"Feel great, too. I don't like getting out of bed in the morning as much as I used to, but I'm probably getting old—"

15

Tuck grinned. "Then I'm getting old, too. How was the passage home?"

"Not bad. They don't jockey those ships around like they once did—steady, responsible hands at the wheel, you know, now that the Mars-Earth run is just a trip around the block. Feels fine to be back Earthside, though—those ships have plenty of good clean air and all that, but there's nothing to compare with a breeze in off the ocean."

"And the Mars job is all finished? Everything done, and you can stay home for a while now?" Tuck's eyes were eager. "Just think, we could spend the whole summer here in New York, and maybe we could get in a fishing trip up North, if you could get away. Remember how we used to fish, Dad?"

"Yes, I remember. I could never forget." The Colonel's face was suddenly grave, and he started down into the taxi terminal, effectively cutting off further conversation. Minutes later they were settling back in the taxi seat, waiting for the little jet car to pull out of the terminal into the broad Middle Level thoroughfare. Finally the Colonel said, "I know a quiet place for supper. You were on your way up to Catskill for the Exhibit, weren't you?"

Tuck nodded enthusiastically. "That's right. The Forty-Seventh International Rocketry Exhibition. I've heard it's really great this year. They're showing all the latest model Interplanetaries, and I've also heard that they're exhibiting the blueprints of the big Venus converter plant." He looked up at his father. "They're also making formal announcements of the Polytechnic Institute scholarship winners for this year—'

Colonel Benedict looked up sharply. "Scholarship winners?"

Tuck nodded. "All tuition and expenses paid for five years of study, and a guaranteed position in mechanics, engineering, or research when you're through. You remember—I wrote you about the competition. I took the

16

qualifying exams in March, and they've already notified the winners informally—"

The Colonel's eyes were wide. "Do you mean—"

Tuck handed him the letter, his face glowing. "This came the day before graduation. I got one, Dad. No hitches, nothing to go wrong. I can start with the incoming class in September."

The Colonel took the letter, and read it very carefully, then reread it. When he finally looked up, his face held a curious expression. "That's great, son—I'm proud of you. I—I really am."

"Well, you don't sound very proud!"

"Believe me, I am, even if I don't sound it. I know how much you wanted it." He stared at the letter, and his face suddenly looked very tired.

"Dad, what's wrong?"

After a long moment the Colonel looked at Tuck, and grinned. "Let's wait until after supper," he said finally. "Then we can talk it over."

The dinner was top-rate, but Tuck couldn't enjoy a bite of it. His father valiantly managed to keep the conversation on light subjects, commenting on the problem of keeping the feet warm on Mars, talking about the new plan for extension of the Rolling Roads, inquiring about the summer's baseball line-up, waxing enthusiastic about the plans for an underwater freight conveyer to Europe—talking of a dozen things while Tuck sat silent, a thousand doubts plaguing him and spoiling the taste of the food. Finally he could stand it no longer. "You've got bad news, Dad. Let's have it."

The Colonel's face was grave. "Oh, not *bad* news, exactly. Maybe you'd call it disappointing news, is all. I'm not home to stay, son. Not even for a week or so. And I can't take in the Exhibition with you. I'm leaving on assignment day after tomorrow, and I may not be back for a long, long time—"

Tuck's eyes grew wide. "But, Dad! They promised

17

you a rest when you got through on Mars! You know they did—"

"I know, but trouble doesn't wait for people to rest. If trouble comes up, someone has to take care of it, and the Security Commission thinks I'm the one to handle this. For that matter, that's why the Mars job was finished so quickly. Major Cormack came out to relieve me. There's more important trouble elsewhere that needs attention."

Tuck's face was stricken. "But where?"

The Colonel hesitated for a moment. Then he said: "On Titan."

Tuck let his spoon drop, staring at his father in disbelief. "On *Titan!* Why, that's clear out to Saturn! Dad, you can't let them send you clear out there—there's nothing out there but one little colony and a half a dozen mines—"

"They're important mines, son."

"How could six lousy mines be so important?"

Colonel Benedict looked at his son for a moment without answering. Then he took a small instrument from his pocket, an old, beaten-up pocket flashlight, pencil-thin, with the bulb shining bravely across the table. "See this? Just a pocket flashlight, the sort that everyone has. As simple a mechanism as you could hope to find, a single bulb and a converter unit. And those lights up there in the ceiling, the bright lights that light the streets—all of them have converter units like this flashlight, drawing their power from the Solar Energy Converters out on Long Island. All the electrical power on the globe, all the heat, all the machinery, all the cars—they all depend on their converter units. Simple power, practically cost-free, power so abundant that the people on Earth can live in luxury. And it's all possible because someone found a way to convert the heat and light of the sun into power to make the world go around—"

"But what does that have to do with your going to Titan?" Tuck protested.

18

The Colonel pointed to the flashlight again. "In that converter unit there's a tiny piece of ruthenium—element number 44, just a little dab of gray metal of the same family as iron and osmium—but an important little dab of metal. It catalyzes the conversion reaction that feeds power to the light. Destroy the ruthenium, and there's no longer any light, no power, no heat. Our whole power supply, our whole civilized world depends on a steady supply of ruthenium." The Colonel looked up at Tuck. "That's what those mines on Titan supply—ruthenium. They take huge quantities of the ore from those mines, and drag out of it tiny amounts of ruthenium. If anything happened to those mines, our entire power supply would collapse. And there's trouble on Titan, trouble in the mines. There's been a great deal of bitterness out there, nasty talk about revolt—oh, nothing that can't be straightened out with a little diplomacy, but it can't wait. It must be done at once, before something really bad breaks loose. That's why the Commission relieved me on Mars."

Tuck's eyes were wide. "But the people who run those mines, Dad—they're convicts, rebels. They can't expect you to go out to such a hole!"

"But they do. I'm to leave in two days. I may not be back for years—" The Colonel fumbled for his pipe, his face very tired.

Tuck watched him for a moment. Then he said, "There was something else—in the taxi, something about the letter."

The Colonel nodded. Carefully, he opened Tuck's acceptance letter, flattened it out on the table. "Yes, I hadn't known about this. When they told me about this mission, I didn't mind the idea of going so very far away, at least not too much—" His eyes caught Tuck's, held them fast. Somewhere a waiter dropped a glass, and the silence clung like a thick, depressing fog. "You see, I was counting on you to go with me."

19

Chapter 2

THERE WAS utter silence for the length of a long breath.
The Colonel quietly lighted his pipe with trembling
fingers, his eyes avoiding Tuck's. Tuck sat motionless,
staring at the sheet of paper on the table top. When he
finally spoke, his words caught in his throat. "I—I can't
go, Dad. I just can't."

"I know. I couldn't expect you to, not with a chance
like this before you."

"Oh, they might give me a leave of absence, but—"
Tuck shook his head miserably. "If there were anything
out there, I could see going—if there were anything at
all. But there's *nothing*—"

"That's right. Nothing but a cramped, dirty, sealed-in
colony, and a few dozen mining tunnels."

"And the colonists—I've heard about them, Dad. There
isn't a soul on Titan worth paying a credit for. They're
troublemakers and traitors, the scum of the Solar System.
Why, every other year they have to send a patrol ship out
there to put down some sort of trouble. They're not
worth it, Dad, living like animals out there—why, they're
hardly *human* any more. They can't be trusted, they're
selfish and treacherous—"

"But they keep the mines going," the Colonel inter-
posed quietly, "and I have to see that nothing interferes
with the mining. If they want to brawl among themselves,
that's up to them. But the mines must keep going."

"Just what kind of 'trouble' is there?"

"Nothing that could be very dangerous. A few missing
supplies to trace down, a few unpleasant rumors to con-

firm or disprove. I might not have to stay more than a few weeks, just long enough to get a good picture of conditions out there to report to the Commission."

Tuck frowned in exasperation. "But aren't there troops out there who can make such a report?"

The Colonel spread his hands. "Not any more. The colonists made it impossible for troops to stay. The last garrison was recalled five years ago."

Tuck lapsed into silence. Somehow, he had known all along that it had been too much to hope for. So much happiness and excitement—something *had* to be wrong. And he knew that his dream of the old life with dad was only a dream. Slowly he looked up at his father's grave face. "I know you want me to go, Dad. But I can't. It would mean postponing the scholarship, maybe losing the chance. I just can't do it. Can you see that?"

"Yes, I can see it." The Colonel knocked out his pipe, a smile crossing his tired face. "I wouldn't expect you to feel otherwise. And after all, I'll be home again—sometime."

Quite suddenly a waitress appeared at the table with a telephone.

"Call for you, Colonel. Will you take it here?"

Colonel Benedict nodded gloomily, and took the receiver. "Benedict speaking—oh, yes, Mac—yes—*tonight!* No, that's impossible. My boy just arrived from L.A.—yes, yes, I know, they should have had the figures this morning—" The Colonel's face went white, and he slowly set his pipe down on the table. "They couldn't be right—but it's idiotic—" He waited a long moment as the voice on the line talked rapidly. Then he said, "All right, I'll be right over. Get the figures together, and get the man who analyzed them down there. See you."

He slapped the receiver down with a bang. "Looks like I can't even have an evening off. Funny figures came in on the Titan supply study, and I'll have to be down at the Commission for a couple of hours." He rose and pulled on his jacket, his face heavy with worry. "Come on, son—I'll put you on a car."

"But is it something serious?"

"Don't know. But don't worry about it. You go up to the apartment and make yourself comfortable. Maybe we can have time to talk later. After all, we've got a lot to catch up on, and darned little time to do it!"

Tuck managed a wan smile, and followed his father's tall figure out to the street. It seemed so unfair, he thought bitterly. There were plenty of Security Commission officers—why must they choose his father for a mission like this? A surface car approached as they reached the street, and Tuck climbed aboard, watching his father's taxi speed out into the Middle Level Thoroughfare downtown.

Ordinarily Tuck would have been excited to be in the city again. He was always thrilled by the tall white towers and the flashing monorails; this was the great business center of the Western World, built to handle the seventeen million people who daily filled the helicopter lanes and Rolling Roads coming into the city. Down on the Lower Level the trucks and busses hummed, the turbines turned, the machinery of the city roared without rest, day and night. Here in the Middle Level where the main highways and monorail trains, and high up above Tuck could glimpse the green terraces and lighted boulevards of the Upper Level, the homes and hotels and apartments, the green parks and the starlighted roofs. Once New York City had been a city of dirt and gloom, of congested traffic and decaying slums. But Solar energy with its great power had made the slums and traffic a thing of the remote past. The city was handsome now, but as the surface car switched to monorail for the Upper Level, Tuck hardly saw the city around him. His mind was filled with anger and bitter disappointment—with a tinge of apprehension thrown in. Titan was a cruel world, so far from Earth, so remote that almost anything might happen. Suppose the trouble was greater than his father suspected? If something went wrong, the Colonel would have little to defend him. And Tuck knew that the laws of common decency would never apply in a sinkhole like the Titan colony.

The car swung out between the rising buildings, and moved swiftly up the open avenue. After a few miles of swift travel, the car left the ground contact, and moved into a neat spiral curve, rising higher and higher, until the open air was overhead. Then the car settled out on the Upper Level rails, and far ahead Tuck could see their apartment building, one of the great towers rising up from the growing darkness below.

The doorman recognized him at once, and welcomed him with open arms. The sight of him cheered Tuck a little. Yes, the apartment was just as he had left it, and his bags had been already sent up. And the Colonel had called, leaving a number where he could be reached if necessary. Tuck walked into the foyer he remembered so well, and soon was zooming up in the elevator to the place he had always known as home.

But happy as he was to see the old familiar places, doubt continued to plague him. The tales he had heard about the mining colony on Titan were hard to forget. He could remember, as a little boy, seeing the crowd of miners and their families, loading aboard one of the great outbound rockets, a drab, surly, mean-looking crew, huddling around their cloth-bound bundles of possessions, their eyes downcast and bitter. His father had explained to him that these people were going out to Titan, the sixth moon of Saturn, and he had been so frightened by their fierce appearance that he had started to cry. He knew now that Titan had not been a penal colony for over a hundred and fifty years, but surely those people must have been desperate. All his life he could remember hearing about the trouble in the mines—murders, piracy, rebellion. And now his father was to go there, to be the only Earthman on the satellite, with the exception of his rocket-ship's crew—

He passed down the bright corridor, stopped before the door to the apartment, and placed his hand palm-down on a shiny metal strip. The admittance panel had been activated to his handprint when he was barely tall enough to reach it; presently the door swung open, and he walked into the darkening apartment, forgetting his doubts in the excitement of being home again.

It was just the same as he remembered it—the entrance, the living-room office, with his father's desk in the corner, complete with visiphone, talkwriter, and the unopened stack of the day's mail, already flooding in, although the Colonel had been home just a day. Tuck crossed the room, and regarded himself in the full-length mirror. He was taller by four inches than he had been the last time he had stood there, and his face was older, more mature, even bearing witness to a somewhat inexpert job of shaving—but the brown hair still stood up in the back, and there was still the wry twinkle in his steady eyes. Not too much change, after all, he thought. He hurried to the window then, threw open the curtains, and stared down at the picture that had always fascinated him, the glowing, beautiful, ever-changing vista of the city at night.

It was fine to be home. Anytime he wanted, during holidays, or whenever he wanted a weekend of rest from his studies, he could come back here. But once the ship blasted for Titan, his father couldn't return again until the job was done, and he was ready for the long trip home—

A cold thought passed through Tuck's mind, and he stopped, coat in hand, staring at the pleasant room. It was a horrible thought, but something deep in his mind was saying over and over: *Suppose he never comes home again? Suppose he's in real danger, suppose he doesn't realize how dangerous the mission is*—Tuck snorted angrily, and hung his coat in the entranceway. It was ridiculous to think such things. Probably the rumors had been exaggerated all out of proportion to the truth.

Anyway, there was no sense thinking about it. He had made his decision, and he would stick by it. And above all, he would get his mind off such nasty speculations. In another day he would be on his way to the Exhibition in Catskill, and he'd have a wonderful reunion with his father in the meantime.

But somehow the prospect of the Exhibition wasn't as exciting as it had been. He walked restlessly about the room, then picked up the pile of letters on his father's desk, and began leafing through them, idly. Possibly some mail had come for him. There was a bill or two, an advertising circular, a large packet from some General, a letter—

Tuck froze, staring at the letter, his heart pounding in his throat. It was an ordinary envelope, small and compact, with the address neatly typed near the center: "Colonel Robert Benedict, 37 West 430th Street, Apartment 944B, Upper New York City, New York." An innocent-looking envelope, just like any one of a dozen his father might receive—

But on the return address was *Tuck's own name*—

Tuck sank down in the chair, staring at the envelope. *He hadn't written any letter*. He hadn't even known that his father would be home. And yet the return read, "Tucker Benedict, Polytechnic Academy School," and the postmark said Palomar, California—

His heart was thumping wildly, and he held the envelope up to the light, tried to make out its contents, but he could see nothing but a dark, opaque rectangle. On impulse he started to pull the plastic opener-tab; then something screamed a warning in his mind. With trembling fingers he held the letter up, staring closely at the opener-tab, just a little piece of plastic, so simple to pull to open the end of the envelope—

Like a cat, Tuck was across the room, fumbling for a razor in his father's desk. In a few seconds he was carefully slitting the envelope down the end opposite the opener, desperately careful not to touch the contents.

The end of the envelope fell open, and he stared in horror at the dull green, slightly luminous plaque inside—

With a cry he carried the envelope at arm's length into the washroom, poured the basin full of water, and dumped the envelope, contents and all, into the water. The green stuff in the envelope crumbled, lost its shape, and became a pasty green-black, evil-looking glob. Tuck ran the water out, and standing as far away as possible, touched a match to the glob.

It flared a little as it burned, making an acrid white smoke, hissing evilly from the dampness. But it burned slowly, and finally crumbled into a soggy ash in the washbowl. Tuck stared at it, his heart pounding in his ears. He had seen a Murexide bomb only once before, in a demonstration at school, but he knew that there was enough high explosive in that innocent-looking envelope to blow his father's head off when he pulled the opener-tab—

And they had used *his name* to booby-trap his own father! The Colonel wouldn't even have had a chance. Angrily, Tuck snatched up the telephone, started to dial Police Headquarters; then quite suddenly he set the receiver down again. Someone was trying to kill his father. There was no other conclusion possible. Someone who hated him enough, or feared him enough, to use a vicious trick like that. Someone had filled the envelope with a Murexide plate, rigged the opener-tab to detonate it, and mailed the letter with Tuck's own name on the return, to make sure the Colonel would open it quickly. Someone had known that the Colonel would be home, that he would be leaving again soon. Someone had known everything, except the single fact that Tuck would be home that night. His father had said that the trouble on Titan was nothing dangerous, nothing but a few rumors, a little unpleasant talk. But the assassin had meant to see that the Colonel never boarded the rocket—

Tuck sat thinking for a long time. The police would

have little to offer, for the Colonel would be leaving in just a day, and then all the police in the world wouldn't be able to help him. And his father *couldn't* realize the danger—he would never have offered to take Tuck with him if he had. And yet, before he even left Earth there had been an attack on his life, carefully planned. What might happen on the rocket, on Titan itself?

A moment later Tuck was on the telephone, waiting for the operator to locate Colonel Benedict, somewhere in the Security Commission conference rooms. At last he heard his father's voice, and he tried frantically to keep his own voice level, to keep his words from choking. "I've been thinking about the trip, Dad," he said. "When did you say your rocket was leaving?"

The Colonel's voice was puzzled. "0800, day after tomorrow. What's the matter, son? Something wrong?"

"No—" Tuck gritted his teeth in the face of the lie. "Nothing wrong. I've just changed my mind, that's all. I've decided to go with you."

Chapter 3

THE LAND OF INCREDIBLE COLD

AN ALARM bell clanged in Tuck's ears, and he sat bolt upright, staring out into the darkness. Then he felt his heart jump as the pilot's deep voice rang out over the public address system: "All hands, muster in landing quarters! Prepare ship for landing! Landing scheduled for 0900 hours—"

Tuck snapped on the cabin wall lamp, and checked his wrist watch. It seemed as if he had barely gotten to sleep; actually, he had slept a full eight-hour period, and his watch read five minutes to eight.

In an hour they would be landing! Excitedly, Tuck dressed, and then threw open the oval-shaped lock to his father's sleeping quarters. "Come on, Dad! We're going down in an hour!"

Colonel Benedict was half dressed, his eyes still blurry from interrupted sleep. "So I hear," he said dryly, rubbing his ear. "I was wondering why they had those speakers built so close to the heads of the bunks."

Tuck took a deep breath, and lifted his feet experimentally. "We're decelerating lots faster, too. I've been feeling like I was sliding out onto the floor for the past six hours."

The Colonel chuckled. "You get used to it, after a while. Let's go forward. The orders for landing are very strict—we'll have to strap down, and prepare for a good jolting." Carefully he packed some gear into a footlocker near his bunk. "We won't be needing these magnetic boots any more—and you might as well store your wrist watch out of harm's way, too. It won't do you any good, once we land. An hour on Titan is only forty minutes long."

Tuck stored his own gear in the footlocker, and together they started up the corridor. There was a breath of excitement throughout the ship. Crewmen were moving swiftly from chamber to chamber, checking the thousand details that must be checked prior to landing operations. Far down in the rear of the ship the engines were whining, and every so often the ship shuddered as the forward and belly jets took hold. Tuck and the Colonel reached the landing bunks, and settled back in the deep, spongy seats, strapping belts tightly around their shoulders and hips as they waited for the landing hour to approach. The tedious journey was nearly at an end.

It had been a long trip out. Even with the powerful atomic engines to accelerate the ship, the journey had taken over two months. For many it might have been dull, but for Tuck it had been wonderful—two long months to become reacquainted with his father, two months to talk, to plan, two months to get used to the idea of once more being father and son. There had been no trouble about the scholarship. The Institute had promised to hold it open for Tuck when he returned, and the journey seemed almost like an incredible vacation trip.

But the time was not spent loafing. Crates of information tapes and microfilm spools had come aboard the rocket before they left, and both Tuck and his father had spent hours every day listening and reading—data and reports on the planet Saturn, studying about her major and minor satellites, reading up on the founding of the colony on Titan, about the working of the mines. Tuck had found the study a little tiresome; he would much rather have spent his time with the pilot and navigator of the ship, and he often managed, on one pretext or another, to turn up in the control room. There he would settle down on the nearest stool, and spend hours

29

listening to the navigator hold forth enthusiastically on the problem of celestial navigation.

But there were many other times when Tuck and his father had sat up in the great plexiglass bay in the nose of the ship, staring out at the black, diamond-studded expanse of space through which the ship sped. They talked of many things, watching Saturn, a tiny dot far in the distance, gradually become bigger, day by day, watching the strange, disklike rings as the planet rotated, one day so far on edge that they were all but invisible, another day surrounding the planet like a halo. Tuck made a game of counting the tiny bright dots circling the planet, the moons of Saturn, considering this an acceptable measure of how close they were coming.

"Hey!" he cried out one day. "I can see another!"

"Where?" The Colonel had peered in the direction Tucker was pointing. "I can't see any that we didn't see yesterday."

"Sure you can—away out, just a little tiny one."

"Right you are! That would be Phoebe, the baby of the lot. Looks like we've counted all nine moons now—"

"I wonder," said Tuck, "why they picked Titan."

The Colonel looked up, and drew out his pipe. "For what?"

"For the mining colony. What was wrong with Japetus, for instance? Or Rhea? They're almost as large as Titan. Why is Titan the only moon of Saturn with a mining colony?"

"Probably because it's richest, among other things. The ore from the Titan mines is very rich—comparatively speaking. Of course, that doesn't mean much, since ruthenium ore is almost as poor in the metal as uranium ore is in uranium. Probably they could have mined Rhea, or Tethys, or any of the other moons, except Japetus—"

"Why not Japetus? It's big enough."

The Colonel chuckled. "You'll also notice that it's half gone. They've never landed on Japetus—the Geiger counters wouldn't let them. The whole moon is radio-active, too hot to toy around with. But when the moons were explored, the explorers spotted a tremendous vein of ruthenium ore running close to the surface on Titan, so they chose that as a likely starting place. And then, Titan is the largest of the nine, the closest to Earth-size of all Saturn's satellites. It's probably as ideal for estab-lishing a permanent colony as any. That's not to say that *any* of them are particularly cozy. Maybe you can't blame people too much for making trouble when they get out there."

Tuck nodded, his conscience giving him a sudden sharp jab. Half a dozen times he had almost blurted out to his father the whole story of the booby trap in the apartment, and then at the last moment held off. It dis-turbed him greatly; he had always been straightforward with dad before, and he knew how hurt the Colonel would be. Sometimes Tuck almost wondered if it had really happened, if he had not made up the whole thing to give himself an excuse to come, but then he would smell that acrid smoke again, see in his mind's eye the sputtering, evil-smelling bomb, stripped of its explosive power, burning in the washbasin. Yet he couldn't bring himself to reveal it, until one day the Colonel had made the overture himself.

It was during one of the observation sessions, near the end of the third week out. It seemed that the Colonel had been watching him that afternoon with far more interest than he watched the stars, and Tuck was becom-ing increasingly nervous. Finally the Colonel said, "When are you going to tell me about it, son?"

Tuck started, his eyes wide. "What do you mean?"

A smile touched the Colonel's lips. "You know what I mean. Your sudden decision to come along with me. *Something* happened to change your mind. I was hoping you'd tell me—"

"Aw, Dad—you wouldn't have let me come, and I *had* to come, after what I found!" Almost tearfully

31

Tuck blurted out the whole story—his worry, the spurious return address, the bomb in the envelope. When he had finished, the Colonel sat still for a long, long time. Then he said, "I wish you'd told me this before."

"I couldn't, Dad. I just couldn't—"

"I know. Sometimes it's the hardest thing in the world." He stared into the darkness. "That puts a different complexion on things, all right. And it begins to make things add up." The Colonel's eyes were grave. "You remember that call I got the evening you came home?"

Tuck nodded unhappily.

"We'd had men checking the invoices on supplies that have been coming out to the Titan colony. We suspected that there has been some funny business—extra supplies, misplaced consignments, 'lost' invoices—but there had never been a double Security Commission check before—"

"You mean there's been smuggling?"

The Colonel nodded. "Food, equipment—tremendous quantities over their quota."

Tuck's eyes widened. "But I thought Security controlled shipments very carefully."

"They're supposed to. But this has been going on for years. All neatly hidden behind such a screen of confusion and inefficiency and red tape that even regular FBI checks couldn't spot it." He shook his head and knocked out his pipe. "Yes, you should have told me about the booby trap—it's bad. The leader of the colony, a man named Anson Torm, knows we're coming. According to the reports, he's one of the biggest troublemakers. And he'll probably be out to meet us when we land." He looked up at Tuck, his eyes filled with concern. "You bit off a mouthful, son. It looks like we're in trouble—real trouble. I only hope it wasn't too big a mouthful."

For a moment Tuck lay still, almost stunned by the terrific jolt. The ship shook from stem to stern, then settled down on its tail in the shallow, rocky crater where supply ships had been landing for over a hundred and fifty years. Carefully Tuck stripped away the straps, examining himself for bruises, and moved forward into the observation bay. Slowly he walked to the great plexiglass window and stared out, hardly daring to breathe.

The sky was dark blue, the darkest, coldest, most hostile blue Tuck had ever seen in his life. The stars stood out like brilliant gems against that blue, and hanging low near the horizon was the huge, luminous globe of Saturn, six times the size of Earth's moon, her rings forming a razor-sharp line around her silvery middle. She was tilted slightly, so that she looked like a huge, off-center top, hanging in the sky. But it wasn't the immense, luminous beauty of Saturn that made Tuck gasp. It was the utter, unbroken desolation of Titan that sent a chill down his back. The surface of the planetoid looked utterly dead.

If there had been a howling wind swirling around the ship, it wouldn't have been so bad. But there was no sound, no motion. The ship's silvery nose rose high above the ground, but on three sides of her were huge black crags jutting up sheer and barren against the cold blue sky. The ground was covered with a blanket of glistening white, covering the jagged rocks, giving way to crevices that sliced deep into the black crater floor. As far as Tuck's eyes could see there was no change, no difference—only the endless succession of jagged rocks, sheer cliffs, and vast gorges, reflecting the pale bluish sunlight from their harsh faces.

"It looks so cold," Tuck murmured.

"It is cold," replied the Colonel, at his elbow. "It's incredibly cold. There aren't words to describe how horribly cold it is, and the cold goes right down to the core of the planetoid."

"But what temperature is it out there? That looks like fresh-fallen snow—"

"Well—it *is* snow, in a way. And it might have been fresh-fallen ten million years ago—we don't have any way of telling. Part of it is water vapor, frozen before it ever became water. Part of it is carbon dioxide, and part is frozen ammonia. And the atmosphere is almost all methane, with a little ammonia and cyanogen mixed in. It's more than 250° below zero out there—"

Tuck stared, hardly believing his eyes. "Is the whole planet like this?" He pointed to the ragged, impossible tumult of rocks and crevices. "It's—amazing."

"The geologists have had a field day studying the surface. They say some of those crevices go down for miles. They're probably volcanic in origin, judging from the type of rock. Or maybe there were Titanquakes, millions of years ago."

Tuck shook his head, still scanning the jagged horizon. "Gee," he said suddenly.

"What?"

"Suppose a ship crashed out here somewhere. It would be lost for good."

The Colonel nodded. "It happened, once."

"You're kidding!" Tuck looked horrified.

"No such thing. Back in the days before the colony, it happened. Exploratory ship, instruments fouled. It crashed out in that wilderness, somewhere, and they never found it. Probably smashed to smithereens on the rocks. They're more careful, nowadays—"

The navigator popped into the room. "Something for you to see, Colonel." He handed the Colonel a pair of binoculars. "Over there to the left."

The Colonel stared through the binoculars for a moment. "Well, well," he murmured, handing Tuck the glasses. "See what you see."

At first Tuck saw the same picture he had seen before —great black rocks, gorges, sheer cliffs. Then his eyes caught something moving, far in the distance, something that looked like a small black bug, crawling up through one of the gorges, slowly but steadily moving toward the ship. Tuck blinked, stared closer, then looked up in alarm. "That's a half-track, or I'll eat my shirt."

"That won't be necessary. It's a half-track, all right.

Looks as if we're going to have visitors." He took the glasses again, scanning the horizon. "I'd hoped to see the colony from here, but that ridge obscures it. It's only about five miles away."

"But why don't they fly over here, instead of driving that clumsy thing?" Tuck took the glasses again, and found the little machine crossing a level stretch of white, then disappearing behind the nearest ridge of rock.

"Half-track is smarter, in the long run. It doesn't go very fast, but it gets here. The colony probably has some jets, but they're not much good for anything but exploration on this terrain. The half-track has power, and it's heavy, and it can easily be sealed against the atmosphere."

"But what about the colony?"

"It's sealed, too. Plexiglass dome. Not very big, either, considering that there are five hundred people living in the colony, including wives and children. And most of the mine shafts open right up inside the dome."

Quite suddenly the creeping half-track appeared, lumbering over the ridge of rocks surrounding the ship, making its way slowly, carefully, down into the shallow center of the crater where the ship stood. It was a strange-looking vehicle, with fat pillow tires eighteen inches thick in front, and heavy caterpillar treads on the back to drive it. It wasn't exactly what they called it, a half-tractor, and it wasn't nearly so small as it had looked. The whole top part was sealed in with a clear plastic bubble, rounding out over the top where a single figure sat, guiding the car in its path. Tuck squinted, but the dull bluish sunlight reflected from the plastic, and he could not get a clear view.

The pilot stuck his head in the door. "Shall I let him aboard? We ran the crane out when we first landed—"

"Better let him come. If we're to have a welcoming committee, we might as well get things off to a good start. This may be one of Anson Torm's men."

Tuck frowned, watching the half-track move down near the ship and grind to a halt. "Don't you think we'd better have guns ready?" he asked. "You never can tell—"

"I'll leave that up to the crewmen. I want to make arrangements for living quarters in the colony, and see what I can find out at the start about the trouble we've been hearing about. Probably it would be best to be as friendly as possible."

The dome of the half-track suddenly sprang open, and a curious-looking figure struggled out, clumsy in the great padded pressure suit that covered his body. A heavy transparent dome covered the man's head, and he stopped momentarily when he reached the ground to seal the half-track up tightly again. Then he moved toward the ship, and in a moment Tuck heard the crane winches hum with the unaccustomed strain as the man was hauled up to the space-lock.

Moments later the lock opened, and a man walked in, his transparent helmet thrown back. Tuck stared at the man, hardly believing what he saw. He was huge, over six feet tall. Even without the suit he would have looked like a powerfully built man. His hair was thick and sandy, and his cheeks were pale; shaggy brown eyebrows jutted out over ice-blue eyes.

For a long moment the stranger stared coldly at the Colonel and Tuck; then his eyes flashed, and he looked straight at the Colonel. "My name is Anson Torm," he said, in a rich bass voice. "What's yours?"

"Benedict—Robert Benedict. This is my son, Tuck." The Colonel stepped forward, offering his hand. "Take off the suit, and make yourself comfortable. You'll roast if you wear that thing in here." ,

Very briefly the man's eyes flickered over Tuck's face; then he looked back at the Colonel, ignoring the hand. "The supply ship isn't due to arrive for four months yet," he said finally, not making a move.

"This isn't a supply ship."

"Then what is it?"

The Colonel smiled. "Call it an informal check on production in the mines, if you like," he said.

Anson Torm's face darkened. "So you're the trouble shooter that Security was going to send?"

"I'm representing the Earth Security Commission, yes."

Slowly the big man began to peel off his pressure suit. His clothing was coarse, with a multitude of patches and careful repairs, and his heavy face was wrinkled with worry and strain. But there was something arresting about the man's face, something that brought a flicker of warmth to Tuck's mind. Anson Torm looked like a powerful man, and not only in terms of physical strength. There was a light of pride in his eyes, a curious air of fierce bravery about him that the coarsest of clothing could not diminish. He stepped from the suit like a man completely in command of himself and of all those around him, and when he turned to the Colonel, it was as if he were meeting the Security Commission President on his own grounds. "All right—I'm representing the interests of the Titan colonists," he said. "I suggest that we go where we can talk, and without delay. I also suggest that you, sir, talk more sensibly than the last few representatives of Earth Security—"

The Colonel's eyebrows went up in surprise. "You mean you've talked to Security men before this?"

"Until my tongue froze," Anson Torm replied coldly. "You must remember that I've lived in this colony for a very long time. This time, I think it would be wise for us to reach an understanding, and reach it fast. Because if your ship leaves Titan without an agreement that meets with the satisfaction of the Titan colonists, I am afraid Earth has received her last cargo of ruthenium."

The Colonel's eyes widened. "You mean your people are refusing to work the mines?"

"Not at all," said the Titan leader. He looked at the Colonel, and his voice was heavy with weariness. "I mean that there will be no mines left for my people to work."

Chapter 4

"THERE'S TROUBLE AT THE COLONY"

FOR A MOMENT they stood in shocked silence, staring at the big man. The Colonel's face was pale, and all traces of his smile had fled. "If that was meant as a threat, I'm afraid you're talking to the wrong man," he said quietly. "I'm not here to listen to threats. I'm here to collect facts, and to draw my own conclusions on the basis of those facts."

Anson Torm was shaking his head. "That was not a threat. It was a simple statement of fact. I don't care to see the mines shut down—I'll do everything in my power to keep them open. That's why I'm here, to talk to you before you go on to the colony." He eyed Tuck and the pilot with frank hostility. "I'd prefer to talk privately."

The Colonel hesitated for a fraction of a second. Then he nodded. "Would you mind, Tuck? Perhaps you could get the gear ready to go back to the colony." He turned to the pilot. "Tuck and I will plan to go to the colony after I've talked with Mr. Torm. I'd like you and your crew to stay with the ship, at least for the time being. And we'd rather not be disturbed by anyone for a while."

Tuck made his way down the corridor toward the sleeping quarters, trying to make some sense from the colony leader's words. He was shocked by the big man's appearance far more than he realized. Granted that he hadn't been entirely sure of what to expect a colonist to look like—he had had mental pictures of crafty, shifty-eyed, bitter-faced people, more animal than human—after all, that *was* the generally accepted picture back home. But Anson Torm's cold blue eyes could hardly have been called shifty, and far from giving a crafty appearance, he had struck Tuck as the sort of man who would prefer sharp conflict to any kind of trickery. Almost shamefacedly, Tuck realized that he had liked the big man on sight, liked him without any basis whatsoever. Yet Torm, he realized, was a Titan colonist with a record for treachery a mile long; no matter how he looked, he couldn't be trusted.

Swiftly Tuck packed the great pressure-sealed bag that was to be taken back to the colony, impatient for the conference to end. He was eager to move, anxious to get out of the ship, to get his feet on the ground of this strange world. What would the colony be like, how could the people live under a plastic bubble?

An idea struck him suddenly, and he hurried aft and poked his nose into the control room. The pilot was sitting at his desk, working on a pile of reports; he looked up and grinned when he saw Tuck. "Looking for something?"

"Well—maybe. I just had an idea. Do we have pressure suits for the outside here on the ship?"

"Of course. Specially made for the surface of Titan, with built-in heaters."

"How about letting me go outside for a while? I'd like to go up on the ridge and see if I can see the colony."

The pilot shrugged. "No harm in that." He stepped into the corridor, broke open one of the storage bins hanging from the overhead. The suit was bulky, well-padded, with the heating element and compressed oxygen tanks built into a compact unit on the back. "Ever been in one of these things?"

"Oh, sure, I went out with the crew when we had to repair that sprung hull plate, on the way out here."

"That's right. Well, then you know how to handle the palm controls for heat and air conditioning and all. Just remember, though—the oxygen supply will last for eight hours, but you'll probably get cold long before

39

that. Keep an eye on the peripheral circulation gauge, and when it says your feet are getting cold, *come in!* It *means* your feet are getting cold, whether they feel cold or not. And don't hesitate to let out a loud yowl if anything happens. If you rip that suit on the rocks, clamp down the section sealer, and scream bloody murder."

Tuck clambered into the clumsy suit, adjusting the fingertips to the row of buttons on the palm, and made sure he could work the joints with ease. On the surface of Titan the suits were more necessary to keep out the cold and the poisonous atmosphere than to regulate body pressures, but without some care in handling the joints of the suit, he would soon be spread-eagled and helpless. Once securely inside, with the oxygen flow adjusted, he lumbered down the corridor into the lock, waved to the pilot, and dogged down the pressure hatches. The pumps whirred until the pressure registered "even" with the atmospheric pressure of the planetoid's surface; then he opened the outer hatch, and stepped onto the crane.

When he stepped off onto the ground, a wonderful feeling of excitement struck him. For the first time, he was setting foot on another world, a world so alien to the warm, comfortable Earth he knew that it seemed impossible that the two could be in the same universe. This was a cruel, cold world, yet just five miles away was a little nucleus of the same warm Earth that he had left behind, a single oasis in a barren wilderness. Man could not live with the hostile cold of Titan's surface, but they could do the next best thing: adapt part of the surface to conditions they *could* live with. Slowly Tuck walked out on the flat crater floor, turned and looked back at the ship, standing like a slender silver finger against the dark blue sky. The white powder crunched under his feet as he walked, and rose in little whirlwinds around his legs, and though it was only two inches deep, he could feel the unearthly chill under his feet. Glancing down, he saw the frost already forming knee-high on the legs of his suit. But close to the skin of his feet he could feel the soft pads of the thermocouples, constantly registering the temperature of his feet. If the blood flow to his feet slowed below a critical level, the thermocouple would register a danger signal, the signal that all spacemen knew too well, which meant that they must return to the warmth of their ships or their feet would be frozen. Tuck shivered, even in the warmth of his suit. He'd wait until he had a half-track before he strayed too far.

The floor of the crater was covered with small, jagged rocks; he carefully picked his way between them, moving off in the direction of the worn path of the half-track. Perhaps up over the first ridge he would be able to see the colony, if the terrain were smooth enough. The going was rough, but by following the ruts, he was able to make good time. These ruts had been worn by the heavy tread of the half-tracks for the past hundred and fifty years, ever since the colony was built, and since the first of the semiannual supply ships had selected this crater as the closest landing place to the colony that would be safe. How could the colonists dare to close down the mines, even to make such threats, if their food and other living necessities must come by such a precarious pipe line from Earth? It seemed incredible to Tuck as he clambered up the rugged pathway, but he had heard Anson Torm's words, and he had seen the paleness of his father's face. Whatever the answer, the mines were in danger of closing. And that, above all, they had to prevent.

He had almost reached the top of the ridge when he suddenly froze in his tracks, staring at the large black rock in the path before him. Frantically he shook his head, then looked again, and his skin broke into a sweat. But there was no question about what he had seen. Just as he had started to pass it, *the black rock had moved—*

Panic rose up in Tuck's throat, but he stood steady. Then it moved again, and Tuck recoiled in horror. It looked just like all the rest of the black rocks, but it

41

slowly changed shape, and slithered down the grade a few inches, then stopped and lay motionless, like a black rock again. Even as Tuck watched it, he saw the bit of rock that lay under the thing dissolve away, and suck up into it, like ink into a sponge—

And then Tuck remembered the paragraph on one of the microfilms he had read, describing these strange black creatures, an incredible sort of half-living thing with a silicon-based metabolism. The report had called them "clordelkus" and said they were quite harmless, but could dissolve away and suck up almost any kind of silicon rock. Tuck shuddered, starting up in the opposite direction from the creature. Harmless or not, it had given him a horrible start. For the first time he realized, almost with a shock, the true strangeness and desolation of the place. This was a harsh world—what could it mean to live here, actually *live* under a plastic bubble, with a cruel, barren, frozen world on all sides, just waiting for the seal to break? These colonists—how could they feel? How could anyone help but hate a life on such a wasteland, in an outpost so remote that contact with Earth could come but once or twice a year? How could anyone live here, and not become desperate after a while? Suddenly Tuck felt terribly alone. There were so many dangers, so many pitfalls, so many ways they might simply disappear on a world like this—

He had started on toward the ridge again when the whine of a motor came to his ear. Suddenly, from over the ridge there was a flash of silver, and a tiny jet plane swooped in, extremely low, skimming through the thin atmosphere with an angry squeal. Tuck stared open-mouthed at the plane as it swung up, barely missing the ship, then made a great whining arc, and settled smoothly in, dropping like a graceful bird onto the smooth floor of the crater not fifteen yards from the crane. Almost immediately the cockpit swung open, and a space-suited figure clambered out, started swiftly for the crane of the Earth ship. Tuck turned and started back for the ship in alarm, moving as fast as his clumsy suit would allow. The plane was a curious-looking thing, hardly twenty feet long from air-scoop to jet, and was shaped short and squat, for all the world like a rocket lifeboat which had been clumsily rebuilt by an inexpert hand. Tuck stared at it in amazement. The exhaust had been so fragile and pencil-thin that he had hardly believed his eyes when it had slid into a landing—Tuck was thoroughly acquainted with small jets back home, and he'd never seen an exhaust cone like that! He longed to stop and inspect this ship more closely, but the stranger was already at the outer lock of the ship. Quickly Tuck moved to the crane, started up, and then waited for the lock to empty and open again, a hard core of fear in his mind. Finally the door swung open; in a moment he stepped into the corridor of the ship, and then stopped short in surprise.

The stranger was not a man, but a youth, hardly older than himself, a stout, muscular fellow who seemed to be attempting to take the ship by storm, in the face of two very angry crewmen. As the lock closed, Tuck saw one of them motion toward the lock, gun in hand, saying, "I told you they're in conference, and they left orders that they weren't to be disturbed under any circumstances. Now will you get out, or do we have to throw you out?"

"But I've *got* to see him," the boy cried. "Look—it wouldn't hurt you to bang on the door and tell him David is here—he won't eat you—"

"We've got our orders—"

"Orders! Bah! What good are orders? You may be dead in five minutes!" The fellow's excitement was expansive, his voice filling the corridor. "Look, I'm David Torm—the man in there is my father. My *father*, can't you hear that? I've got to see him—" Swiftly the boy's voice became wheedling. "What will it hurt to let me see him for just ten seconds? What can they do to you for that? Hang you by your toes? Or aren't they doing that on Earth any more? Let me see him, and your commander will be forever grateful. You'll be the apple of his eye! Just one moment to see my father, I beg of you—"

The man, who was growing redder by the minute, nearly exploded at this outburst. "You move an inch further into this ship, sonny, and you'll be dead."

The boy's eyes flashed angrily, and he shook his fist in the guard's face. "Hah! You'd not have the nerve to shoot me, you chicken! I'll see my father if I have to slice your ears off, clod! May your suit spring a leak, may your airline clog—*don't lay a hand on me, or you'll regret it—*" The boy's voice rose shrilly, and he ducked nimbly back when the guard took an angry swipe at his head. Swiftly he turned to Tuck, his eyes bright. "*You!* Explain to this dolt, in simple terms, that I've got to see my father before it's too late!" He stared in utter contempt at the crewman, whose face had gone purple, then turned his entire attention to Tuck, as if the man had ceased to exist. "It's urgent," he said quiet seriously. "I must see him."

"Why?" Tuck eyed the youth coldly, fighting down an impulse to laugh aloud at the crewman's discomfort. "They're busy. Why can't you wait?"

David Torm groaned in exasperation, brushing thick blond hair out of his eyes. His face had the same healthy, weathered look as his father's, and the eyes were the same startling blue—but this lad's eyes were quicker, with a twinkle of exuberant mischief in them, not in the least clouded by his excitement. "I've been trying to explain to this toad over here for fifteen minutes. There's trouble at the colony. My father must get back there as soon as possible."

"What kind of trouble?"

The blue eyes flashed in disgust. "You too? Questions, always questions! A clordelkus is attacking. He's chewing up the bubble. In half an hour the colony will be

44

frozen to death. Can't you see it's urgent?" David didn't even crack a smile.

Tuck just looked at him. "So let it chew," he said dryly. "Then maybe *my* father and I can go home."

David Torm's face lighted up. "So it's your father he's talking to! Then tell my father I'm here."

Tuck looked him straight in the eye. "If I thought you'd been telling a word of truth since you got here, I'd do so gladly. Tell me what the trouble is, and I'll tell him."

David threw up his hands in despair. "You Earth people! You're all alike! Stubborn, like mules." He stared at Tuck for a moment, then started to bolt on his helmet again. "If it wouldn't kill you," he said sarcastically, "perhaps you'd tell my father to get back to the colony without losing a minute, as soon as he's through talking. I can't wait, I've got to get back." He started for the lock. "Tell him that Cortell is organizing his group—can you tell him that?" Without waiting for an answer, he clamped down the faceplate of the helmet, still muttering under his breath. Tuck stood watching as the lock door clanged shut, thoroughly confused. Maybe the boy had been serious! There had been something about those pale blue eyes that had demanded trust. But then, he was a colonist, and nothing he said could be trusted. Tuck turned angrily away from the lock. Probably he had come aboard simply to look around—or maybe he had his pockets stuffed with Murexide plates. There was no way of telling. And certainly, it wasn't worth taking a chance.

Impatiently Tuck paced the corridor outside the room where the men were conferring. They had been talking almost two hours now, and as the minutes passed, Tuck became more and more uneasy. Perhaps he should have trusted the boy, accepted his word. Who was Cortell? And what sort of a group was he organizing? Probably Anson Torm would know the significance of that. But surely the conference was more important than anything else. If the mines were to shut down, there would be real trouble, and soon.

Tuck's mind drifted back to the blond-haired youth. So Anson Torm was his father. That meant he must have been born and grown up in the colony. For an instant a thousand questions flooded Tuck's mind, questions he would like to ask. And the jet plane—could David possibly have rebuilt it himself? It would be wonderful to have such a ship, to come and go with as he pleased, just big enough to use for exploratory jaunts— and especially if he lived on such a place as Titan, with so much of the surface still a barren, uncharted jungle of rocks and gorges and black-faced cliffs. But he jerked his thoughts away from such channels; probably he would never even talk to the fellow again, and certainly he'd have no chance to try out his plane. There were more important things to do—

And then the door to the room flew open, and Colonel Benedict stalked out, his face white and drawn with anger. He was followed by the tall colony leader. Anson Torm's face looked very tired, and his jaw was set in a grim line. Tuck stared at the two men, and his heart sank.

The first conference was over.

Chapter 5

- AMBUSH

IN THE COURSE of his eighteen years Tuck Benedict had seen the Colonel in many moods, but he had never before seen such a combination of anger and distrust on his father's face. The Colonel stalked into the room, barely nodding to Tuck, and slapped a sheaf of papers down on the desk furiously. Then he snatched up the intercom speaker, his hand trembling barely within the limits of control. "Better get up here, Jim," he snapped to the pilot. "We're going to the colony."

Tuck stared at his father, and then at the tall colony leader, his heart sinking. What could have happened? His father was furious, and Torm was controlling himself with difficulty, his face white, lips in a tight, grim line. Neither man spoke; Torm was struggling into his pressure suit again, the tired wrinkles deeper around his eyes, an expression of bitterness and disappointment on his face.

Finally the Colonel turned to the tall colony leader. "You have accommodations for us at the colony, I presume?" he said coldly.

Torm shrugged. "If you desire them. You and your son will have to stay in my quarters—there's no place for guests in the colony. But your crew will have to stay here."

The Colonel snorted. "They will, all right." He turned sharply to the pilot who had just come in. "We're leaving for the colony," he said, his voice regaining some semblance of control. "We'll have a hand radio with us, of

47

course, and I'd like a man here on the receiver all the time."

The pilot nodded. "Any idea how long—?"

"None in the least. Maybe a day, maybe six weeks. I couldn't even guess, at this point." He shot a venomous glance at Anson Torm.

Tuck watched the men miserably. The conference had been a failure—obviously. He knew the Colonel had counted on establishing some sort of liaison on the first meeting, some grounds for understanding—and it appeared that he had failed utterly. And Torm had said that unless an understanding was reached, there wouldn't be any mines left to work! Tuck felt a chill run down his spine. What could he have meant? The colonists wouldn't *dare* to stop work, to close down the mines—and yet the colonists were violent—rebels and traitors. They might dare anything. Tuck's heart skipped a beat as he thought of David Torm's visit to the ship, and his message suddenly took on a horrible significance. If there had been some plan made, back at the colony, to start a violent outbreak if the conference was not successful —Tuck turned to Anson Torm in alarm. "Your son was here—"

The colony leader lowered his hands from the suit slowly, staring at Tuck, his pale blue eyes widening. "David? You mean he came here to the ship?"

Tuck nodded. "Half an hour ago. He wanted to see you, but we told him you'd left orders not to be disturbed."

There was alarm on Anson Torm's face now, and he blinked at Tuck. and then shot a glance at the Colonel. "What did he want?"

"He wouldn't tell me. Said there was trouble of some sort back at the colony—"

"Cortell!" The word was like a curse.

Tuck nodded excitedly. "That's right. He said Cortell was organizing his group, or something like that, and that you should get back as soon as possible."

Anson Torm scowled, his fist clenching at his side. "Did he say anything else?"

"Nothing else. He just left in a hurry."

Torm half-turned to the Colonel, worried lines furrowing his broad forehead. "This is a horse of a different color," he said sharply. "I think you'd better let me go in alone—before you come."

The Colonel's eyebrows lifted. "Not on your life," he growled. "Not after the story you've been telling me for the last two hours—"

Anson Torm's eyes flashed. "Colonel, *you've got to trust me*. For the sake of the mines, and for the sake of your own neck. This is something I've got to handle alone—"

"I'd say you've handled it rather badly alone." The Colonel's voice lashed angrily. "Who is this Cortell?"

"I told you about John Cortell. He's a troublemaker, and he's dangerous."

The Colonel regarded Torm for a long moment. Then he said coldly, "I thought *you* were supposed to be the leader of the colony people."

Torm's mouth tightened. "I am."

"Then why don't you keep your troublemakers in confinement where they belong?"

"Colonel, you simply don't understand the situation at the colony—"

"That's for dead sure!" The Colonel cut him off with a wave of the hand. "I don't understand a thing you've said all afternoon. And that is precisely why I'm not going to stay here now. All I've heard is double talk and threats. You want to keep the mines working, but you don't want to keep the mines working. You've gotten extra supplies, but you haven't gotten extra supplies. You're the colony leader, but you can't lead the colony! Bah!" The Colonel's face was red with anger. "I want to know what's going on out here, and I've had nothing but nonsense handed to me. Now I want the facts. If there's trouble in the colony that you can't control, we'll

49

see what the trouble is, and we'll see if *we* can't control it."

"You're determined to go in with me?"

"I am indeed."

Torm shrugged his shoulders, angrily. "Then you'd better hurry, because I'm going in as fast as I can get there." He turned back to the pressure suit, and Tuck was almost startled to see the whiteness of his face. The Colonel turned to Tuck, his voice quieter. "Maybe you'd better stay, if there's likely to be trouble—"

"If there's trouble, you'll need help," Tuck protested. "Anyway, they won't dare harm us—not with the crew as close as it is, and you with Security credentials—"

The Colonel frowned for a moment, then nodded. "All right. But you'd better be quick about it—"

A few moments later they were standing in the lock, waiting as atmosphere hissed out of the exhaust pumps until the outer door sprang open. The crane grated shrilly as they descended, and Tuck felt his blood stir as they approached the ground. Now, at last, he would be seeing this strange colony for himself. The people who lived in a bubble! He shook his head, still puzzled that people would choose to live in such a time-forgotten outpost. What could be driving them? And yet, he knew, they seldom came back to Earth, once they had worked on Titan. Occasionally they came back, looking for work, applying to the schools, or just vacationing, but almost invariably a Titan colonist who came back to Earth for any reason was back on the next ship out to Titan again. Of course, everyone knew that they were poor workmen, shifty and lazy and treacherous, and nobody on Earth wanted to hire a man who knew nothing but how to keep methane out of a mining tunnel, and there probably wasn't a person in the colony who could qualify for entrance requirements at an Earthside University—and with their long history of treachery and violence, who wanted them back on Earth anyway? They couldn't even run their own tiny colony without constant fighting and revolutionary outbreaks—what place could they find in the civilized society back on Earth?

The three of them reached the floor of the crater, and stepped off the crane, clambering into the cockpit of the half-track. The motor started, and the vehicle gave a lurch, and rolled in a wide arc, crawling over the ragged terrain like a short, stubby worm, absorbing the bumps and declivities with the pillow tires and the caterpillar treads that gave the thing its driving power. Tuck caught a brief glimpse of the tall, slender ship, and then it disappeared as the half-track made a complete circle and started up toward the first ridge of crags. Tuck felt a sudden pang of uneasiness pass through him. At least in the ship there had been a certain degree of safety. But beyond that ridge of rocks—who could say? It was no use fooling himself. They were leaving their safety behind.

He heard his father's voice in the earphones, a startling sound, as though the Colonel were speaking directly into his ear. "Did the boy say what Cortell was trying to organize?"

"Not a word. He clammed up the minute I asked. Maybe you should ask Mr. Torm. He seems to know what his son was talking about."

Anson Torm threw a glance at Tuck, then met the Colonel's cold eyes. "I think you'll want to find out for yourself," he said coolly. "John Cortell is powerful—and he's getting more powerful every day. He has a lot of colonists on his side, and he wants open revolt with Earth. I've been trying to tell you for the past two hours that the colonists have reached the end of their tether out here. They want some changes made, and they're going to have those changes. And if they find out that you've come here without any idea of making changes, I can't vouch for what will happen."

The Colonel raised his eyebrows in exasperation. "And I told you, Security can't consider making changes unless we know exactly what is going on in this colony.

51

All the Earth asks is the colonists' cooperation—nothing more."

Torm snorted. "Co-operation! The Earth doesn't want co-operation, the Earth wants slaves! We've co-operated to the limit, and we've been slapped in the face every time. We've dealt squarely with Earth, and they've cheated us and betrayed us and degraded us—"

"And I suppose that these smuggled supplies are part of your policy of dealing squarely with Earth?"

Torm's face was white. "You've been given the wrong information about our supplies. That's all I can say." He swung the wheel of the half-track sharply to avoid a huge rock, and the car shook as if every bolt were about to fall loose.

The Colonel's eyes were dark. "I'm afraid that answer won't do this time, Torm. Security made the investigation this time, in duplicate—two separate groups working independently, checking shipping orders, receipts, invoices; checking rocket schedules and loading lists and everything else. They both came up with the same results. Oh, the shipping was well concealed—changing suppliers every couple of years, filling duplicate orders—always above quota, extra supplies. No colony in the Universe would need the supplies this colony has been piling in for the last hundred years—"

Torm looked straight at Colonel Benedict, and his face was grave. "But I tell you in all truth that we've received nothing in this colony that we don't need—for survival."

"You mean you need food enough to feed twice your population?" the Colonel snapped. "What are you doing to that food? Are you trying to tell me that just working these mines requires almost double the normal food supply?"

"I repeat—we have received nothing that we don't need—*for survival*." It seemed to Tuck that the colony leader placed an emphasis on the last two words. "And you must remember that the men are working, they

52

spend their days in physical labor, they need more food than the average Earthman. And you aren't dealing with the same conditions here as on Earth. We have atmosphere leaks to plague us, we have contamination problems. When food gets contaminated with some of the natural bacteria flora here, or when our hydroponics are thrown out of balance by natural fungi, we can't take any chances. We have to throw out all we have that may have been contaminated, or run the risk of a plague, or of no oxygen to breathe—"

"And I suppose your people eat *metal*, Mr. Torm? I suppose they eat tool steel? Or does the strange Titan atmosphere make your tools and machinery more prone to breakage?"

The colony leader gripped the steering bar heavily, not even answering. The half-track reached the top of the grade, and for a brief moment they could see the colony, far ahead, a small, grayish, glasslike bubble, sitting down in a valley between two long lines of jagged peaks. Tuck stared, open-mouthed at the picture, until the half-track went over the ridge and started bumping and jogging down the other side, down a sharp ravine of jagged rock. Torm picked his way carefully, partly following the path that had been worn by generations of supply trains crossing the rocks to the colony, partly moving aside from the path to avoid boulders of black rock which had fallen onto the path from the vibrations. The whole landscape had a strange, uncertain appearance; the rocks did not look stable, they did not appear solid and timeless like the jutting slabs of rock Tuck had seen during his summer climbing adventures in the Rocky Mountains on Earth. These rocks looked sharp, precariously balanced; they jutted up stark and barren, leaning crazily, looking for all the world as if they had been dropped there, quite suddenly, by some celestial hand, and then stopped in motion before they had a chance to roll. The half-track struck one of the boulders near the path a glancing blow, and then Torm slammed on the brakes as the boulder went crashing down the slope before them, bouncing like a huge, crazy black ball until it struck the bottom, bringing down a shower of pebbles and debris after it. Without a word Torm started the machine again, lumbering carefully down the slope. About a mile ahead was a narrow cleft or gorge between two cliffs; the half-track rumbled toward it.

Then, quite suddenly, the men heard an unearthly screech in their ears, and the little jet plane zoomed in close over them, turned a flip, and zoomed back, still closer. The Colonel stared at the plane as it skimmed over, not twenty feet above them, and then turned to Torm in alarm. "What was that?"

Torm frowned, staring through the plaxiglass panel at the little plane as it made a graceful arc in the sky, and raced down in front of them, zigzagging across their path. "That's odd," he said. "That's my son's ship. An old lifeboat he begged off one of the supply ships and rebuilt for an exploring scooter. But I don't know what he's trying to do—"

The ship was indeed behaving most oddly. It swooped down swiftly, coming so close that the men in the half-track gripped their supports, half-expecting it to crash into their top; then it whizzed over and sped for a hundred yards or so down along the valley floor before them, zigzagging across their path as before. The huge cleft between the cliffs ahead was closer now, and the half-track lumbered along the path, with the little jet doing its strange maneuverings ahead of them as they went.

"What *is* he trying to do—signal us?" The Colonel was half out of his seat as the plane zoomed overhead again.

Torm shook his head. "I-I don't think so. He'd drop a flare if he wanted us to stop—"

"Well, he's going to kill us—*look at that!*"

The plane almost struck the valley floor that time. Torm's breath hissed between his teeth, and his foot slammed down on the brake as the little jet plunged down to what appeared almost certain disaster; then, quite suddenly, it lifted itself again, and zipped up high through the gorge ahead. Torm muttered something under his breath, his face dark.

"He's crazy!" the Colonel breathed.

"He's up to something." Torm shook his head again as the half-track skidded down a bank toward the gorge. "He's a skillful flier, but he knows better than that."

"But what—" The plane had circled around and made another run through the cleft, somewhat lower, and on less of an angle than the first.

Tuck had been staring at the plane silently for several minutes. "Looks to me like he's scouting the path for us!" he exclaimed suddenly. "Didn't you see that? He's cutting in as low as he dares, and zigzagging along the floor—"

"But that's ridiculous. There's nothing—"

The Colonel leaned forward sharply. "Tuck's right," he said. "He *is* scouting—"

The little jet had just made another run through the cleft, not a hundred yards ahead of them, and started down into the valley below. Then, almost as an afterthought, David brought the ship up high, and raced over behind the half-track. With a whine the ship skimmed along the racine, quite low, and then zoomed down until it almost touched the ground; suddenly it swung directly into the half-track's path, and buzzed through the gorge ahead of them, not four feet off the ground—

And on the tail of the jet there was a blinding, purple flash, and a huge roar, and the entire gorge went up in a fury of purple fire and gray-white smoke. In horrible slow-motion, the cliffs on either side of the gorge crumbled from the concussion, heaping tons of rock down into the pathway, in the exact spot where the half-track would have been just a few minutes later. The concussion wave caught the jet as it zipped through, and the little plane went into a series of sickening rolls, then panned out and slid into a crash landing somewhere behind the pillar of fire and smoke that was rising from the gorge—

Torm slammed on his brakes, and shoved the half-track into reverse, his face white as putty. Frantically he backed the machine away from the pillar of fury in the gorge and started it up a flanking path, up a sharp declevity that would take it around the gorge to the right. Tuck held on with both hands as the half-track clambered up the unbroken path, engines roaring, bouncing all its occupants about the inside like dolls in a box, but Anson Torm wrestled the steering bar, gunning the machine as fast as he could make it go. At the top of the rock he slowed, spotted the scooter lying with a crumpled wing and a split-open jet, on the floor of the gorge below the place of the explosion. Torm turned the half-track in that direction, and it roared on down the hill. All three of them watched the wreck, but there was no sign of life from the little scooter. It seemed a lifetime as the half-track made its way down; as they came closer, Tuck felt his stomach muscles tighten. Somehow, David must have known that an ambush might be planned to destroy the half-track as it returned from the ship; when he'd not been allowed to see his father, he had waited, then scouted the pathway for them as they made their way back to the colony. Tuck suddenly felt sick—David had been telling the truth, there on the ship! And Tuck had had to pick that time to be stuffy and suspicious. And he had thought himself very clever the way he had handled the flamboyant visitor! Quite suddenly and incredibly, as they moved down toward the wreckage of the jet plane, Tuck felt deeply ashamed. The blond-haired lad had had the courage to risk his own life to save them from a trap—and now he was down there in the smashed jet—

They reached an outcropping above the jet scooter, and Torm was out of the half-track in an instant. The Colonel and Tuck followed, staring at the crumpled wing and smashed-in undercarriage of the little ship. And then, even as they approached, the cockpit flew open, and David appeared, moving feebly, dragging himself up out of the seat. Torm let out a cry, and helped him down to the ground, checking his helmet for leaks as the boy muttered incoherently. Then David's knees buckled under him, and they eased him down to the ground.

"It's unbelievable," Torm said, his voice choking. "He's alive. And no bones broken—probably just a slight concussion." He motioned toward the half-track, and together they carried the youth, pressure suit and all, into the cab of the machine, made a place for him on the floor behind the seats where some oilcans had been stored. They were silent; as they moved the lad, the anger in Anson Torm's face grew like a gathering storm. "They did it this time," he muttered as he took his place behind the controls of the half-track. "They went a step too far this time. If it hadn't been for David they'd have gotten all of us—"

The Colonel stared at Torm, wide-eyed, and there was bewilderment on his face. "I don't get this," he said. "I can see somebody ambushing *us*—Tuck and me—but *you* were in this half-track too—"

Torm's eyes were filled with bitter anger. "A remarkable observation," he said sourly. "Now maybe you'll believe me when I tell you I'm on your side. This was well-planned—magnetic fuse on a land mine, so that anything metallic that came into that gorge would be gone. Beautiful. Even David missed it, until he brought the scooter in at the same level as the half-track. And it was supposed to kill two birds with one stone." He turned a bitter grin toward the Colonel and Tuck. "Or maybe I should say three birds—"

"And you know who planted the trap?"

Torm looked up again, and his eyes were not pleasant. "Yes, I know who did it. And I know what to do about it. I think it's time for a showdown with John Cortell."

Chapter 6

THE PRISONER

THE COLONY lay tight and compact in the long, shallow valley between the two parallel lines of black, jagged peaks. A queer, bulbous, glistening bubble of heavy plexiglass surrounded the entire outpost like an alien cocoon. Tuck stared at the huge bubble wonderingly as the half-track rumbled the last hundred yards down the grade toward the entrance lock. "You mean that that plastic stuff covers the entire colony?"

Anson Torm nodded grimly. "Every crack and leak is sealed off with the stuff, or with the plastic gum we use to seal off and caulk leaks. Remember, we're human beings—we're not equipped to live and breathe in a methane atmosphere at 250 degrees below zero." He swung the half-track around a heap of rocks, and rumbled up to the opening of the lock. Tuck peered with excitement through the glimmering sheathing. The pale sun was almost below the horizon, and the colony bubble caught the dim, ghostly light of Saturn, now almost directly overhead. Inside the dome Tuck could see the pale electric lights beginning to glow, brightening the drab interior as much as anything could brighten the dreary place. The half-track moved into the lock, and Torm began loosening his pressure-suit helmet almost at once, the anger still black on his tired face. Suddenly the inner lock-hatch opened with a loud ping, and the half-track moved forward until the door could close behind it. Torm threw open the top, and sprang out onto the ground.

Tuck followed Torm out, holding up a hand to help his father, his eyes taking in the street in all its details. It was a strange street; the lock opened into a large, clear area, faced by a long, low building of rock and wood that looked like a troops' barracks. The clearing stretched out to the left and right in a rough unpaved road that curved around, following the course of the curved dome. And lining the road on both sides were strange-looking buildings, mostly thrown together of black stones and coarse mortar—buildings doubly strange because they seemed to have no roofs. The rock walls rose eight or ten feet in the air to end in jagged wall-like tops; on a few Tuck could see brightly colored woven blankets and painted canvas thrown across the tops, but many had nothing of the sort, and through one open door Tuck could see the bright dome shining through from above.

Near the lock, one of the buildings had a large porch-like arrangement, and signs were posted on the black walls—obviously a trading post or store. Several men and women were gathered on the porch, staring at Tuck and his father with dark, suspicious eyes, and a group of children were chattering and pointing. Then a small, deeply tanned man broke from the group and ran across the clearing toward them. He ignored the Earthmen as if they weren't there, and turned to Anson Torm excitedly. "What happened, Anson? We heard a blast—"

Torm nodded to the man, and gestured toward Tuck and his father. "The Earth delegation, Ned. Colonel Robert Benedict and his son, Tucker. This is Ned Miller."

The little colonist looked up at the Colonel and Tuck with sharp brown eyes, as if he were trying to penetrate a veil; then he sniffed in disgust and turned back to Torm. "Now I think that's real nice," he said sourly. "But what—" His eye caught sight of the boy in the back of the half-track. "Anson! That's David—what happened, man?"

They helped David out of the cab onto the ground,

where he sat, still limp. The man called Ned Miller galvanized into frantic action, waving a couple of the men over, shouting for a stretcher. "We heard the blast half an hour ago," he said excitedly. "We expected David to be back with some news, but he didn't come. Is he hurt bad?"

"Not bad. Concussion, or maybe just shaken up a little." He turned to one of the men. "Send over word to Doc Taber, and ask him to come running, will you?"

"But what happened?" Ned Miller asked again.

Torm's face darkened as he stood up. "Ambush. One of the mining charges, with a magnetic fuse. David must have gotten wind of it, somehow. He came over in the *Snooper*, and scouted it out for us—over in Carter's gorge. Didn't touch us, but the concussion wave got the *Snooper* and David."

Ned Miller scowled, rubbing his grizzled chin. "Cortell," he said.

"Who else? But there's no proof."

"Proof, bah!" Miller exploded, his brown eyes snapping. "Cortell couldn't wait for you to get out of here this morning. He and about ten men had a meeting, a quarter of an hour after you left, and half a dozen of his boys were out of the mines this afternoon."

Torm nodded angrily. "Send Martz and Darly to get Cortell down to the convention room, and pronto. Legal order. We'll be down there in a few minutes, and we want him there. And if he doesn't want to come, break his legs and then bring him."

Miller's eyes were worried. "There'll be trouble, Anson. Unless you and the Colonel got farther than I think you did—"

"There'll be trouble, all right. But there isn't much we can do about it now. This thing has got to stop." He turned to find the short, balding figure of the colony's doctor kneeling beside David.

"What about it, Doc?"

The doctor examined the boy's head carefully. "Better

get X-rays. I wouldn't worry, but he'll be down at the infirmary for a couple of days. Check with me later."

Anson nodded, and turned to Tuck and the Colonel. Together, they started across the clearing into the long, low building that faced them.

It was a barracks, on either side of the large common room—the quarters of the former military contingent, now used as a storehouse. But in the rear were stone steps, leading down in a long spiral. Anson Torm snapped on lights, his face still tense with anger, and they started down. A number of the colonists were in the common room reading, and a few waved at Anson as they passed through—but there were no smiles when they saw Torm's company. At the bottom of the stairs they found themselves in a huge underground excavation, filled with rude seats, with a desk and chair at the front, and a massive wall of files. Anson Torm nodded Tuck and the Colonel into seats, then seated himself at the table, and waited, drumming his hand on the table top in impatient anger. The hall was dark, and very silent. There was room here to seat every one of the colonists, man, woman, and child, but now the room was empty. Yet, if he listened closely, Tuck could hear more clearly the strange, rumbling noise he had heard up above, coming from far underground—a persistent sound that never dropped nor rose, and almost became a part of the background of the place. Probably pumps, Tuck reasoned—or maybe mining machinery. Whatever it was, it only added to the gloom of the place. Tuck shifted uneasily, wishing the stillness were not so complete.

Finally Colonel Benedict broke the silence. He turned to Anson Torm questioningly. "What do you propose to do with this Cortell person when he gets here?"

Torm turned his angry eyes to the Earthman. "I don't know," he said slowly.

"You mean you'd let him get away with something like this?" The Colonel's eyes were wide.

"Like what?"

61

"Like an ambush. Like attempted murder." The Colonel's voice was tense.

Torm stared at him tiredly. "I may have no choice. I am the elected leader of this colony—nothing more. I have the position of judiciary—the power to select juries and the power to make final judgments in judicial matters of law. And since I've held this position, I've studied Earth law and colony law for a long, long time." The big man shrugged his shoulders apologetically. "Unfortunately, in all this time and study, I've not yet found any justification for condemning a man with no evidence against him."

"But everyone here seems to know that it was Cortell who planted the trap—or at least Cortell's men—"

"This may very well be true. But it's not proof."

The Colonel drummed the table top impatiently. "And yet, from a very selfish viewpoint, that was a deliberate attempt on my life—nothing more nor less. I'm here with a job to do—and I intend to see it done, if I have to take Cortell, and you, and everyone else involved in the little plot and place them under Earth arrest for high treason."

Torm looked at the Colonel for a long moment, studying his face, a look of puzzlement in the colony leader's eyes. "You forget one thing," he said finally. "It was an attempt on *my* life, too. And it nearly killed my son."

"But why on *your* life?"

Ansom Torm leaned forward, his eyes square on the Colonel's face. "How well do you know the history of this colony?"

"Quite well, I should say—"

"Security Commission records, no doubt."

The Colonel reddened. "Among other source materials. What are you getting at?"

"It was started as a prison, this colony," Torm said. "That was a hundred and fifty years ago. A place where criminals against Earth society were sent, a deathtrap, a modern-world Devil's Island if you wish—You've heard of that place, I presume? Not a fair comparison, really—at least those poor creatures had Earth sky and Earth sea—" The big man's eyes grew wistful for just a moment. "But back when the colony here was started, ruthenium wasn't so critical to Earth economy. As time went on, Earth authorities began to realize that they didn't *dare* leave the mining of their ruthenium up to criminals and cutthroats, so they recruited workers, made the mines a free colony, and started the mining system that we have here now—"

"This is all very interesting," the Colonel said. "But I repeat—what are you driving at?"

Tuck watched the colony leader closely. He felt the awkwardness between the two men quite acutely. And strangely, as he listened, the doubts which had been creeping into his mind since his first sight of the big man's face on the ship became stronger. It seemed incredible that this quiet voice, this stern face with the lines of worry and compassion engraved over the years, could be the voice and face of an outlaw and a liar. And yet he knew, even thinking it otherwise was fool-hardy. There had been two vicious attacks, there was violence in the very air of this strange colony, and this big, sandy-haired man was the leader here. Or at least, he claimed to be—

Torm held up his hand. "Patience, Colonel. Think about history for a minute. Earth made Titan a free colony, which was very fine—except that the people on Earth could never forget that it was originally a prison colony. Ruthenium became more and more necessary to the growing luxury on Earth, and this colony became more and more vital—and the people on Earth grew more and more afraid of us who worked in the mines. They were afraid of the power we might assume, they were afraid we might someday grow too strong. So, you see, they took steps to see that we would never grow too strong. Very gradually, very skillfully, they turned propaganda on Earth against us—propaganda deliberately planned to degrade us as human beings, planned to lower our status, planned to make people on Earth more afraid of us, to make them regard us as slaves, half-animals, rebels—"

Colonel Benedict stared at the colony leader. "You're expecting me to believe this?"

"You should believe it," Torm replied softly. "Your own Earth Security Commission has engineered it for years—"

"The Commission is responsible for the security of people on Earth—nothing more. They hardly have the time to set themselves up as persecutors. There's been trouble in this colony for years—you know that as well as I. Time after time Earth delegations have come out here, trying to reach a ground for peace and co-operation. Time after time they've been met with treachery and hatred."

"That is not true, Colonel. You have been afraid of us, and naturally we have grown to fear you, too. After all, Earth has the power to starve us, to smother us, to slaughter us, if they wish." The colony leader stood up, walked back and forth in the still room. "We know that. We're helpless out here, alone, utterly dependent on Earth's regular supplies. But we have always known how much Earth needs ruthenium. Of course they have never done us physical harm—but there are other things that can destroy people, Colonel. Men must be able to keep their self-respect, and the respect of the people they live with. And slowly, over the years, we've been down-graded in the eyes of Earth people. Oh, nothing deliberate or premeditated—but we've lost our status as citizens in the Solar System. Promises have been broken, supply quotas have been lowered, higher and higher production has been expected, and every year our position as citizens falls, and fear builds up, and we go through the same vicious circle again."

Tuck stared at Torm, hardly believing his ears. This was seditious talk; this was treason—yet his father sat

64

calmly, without even lifting a finger to stop the man. Finally, when Torm had finished, the Colonel said, "Let's get to the point, Mr. Torm. Where does Cortell come into this?"

Torm shrugged. "The people of the colony have taken all they're going to take. They've had enough for decades, but they never had anyone smart enough to lead them, or think for them. But Cortell is a clever man— far more clever than I am, Colonel. He knows how to use propaganda and back-street whispers. He's an incendiary, third generation in this colony, and he hates Earth and Earthmen. There are many people here who have been listening to his talk, more and more, and he's set about deliberately to undermine my power as leader. My power is traditional here, and it's elective. And Cortell pretends to believe that by open revolt the colony can win against Earth, and dictate its own terms—"

The Colonel jerked back in his chair, staring. "Open revolt—you mean armed warfare against Earth?"

"Precisely."

"Why, that's ridiculous! The Earth could—"

"The Earth could bring its bombing rockets and wipe out the colony in an hour," said Torm quietly. "But it would be too late, because Cortell could do his work much more quickly than Earth could move. Because the first step in open revolt, as Cortell sees it, would be to break open the mining tunnels, flood the mines with methane, and then set a match to it—" The colony leader looked up slowly. "Methane and oxygen explode," he said softly. "They explode with such violence that no one would ever again be able to operate these mines."

Colonel Benedict chewed his lip. Then he looked up at Torm. "And where do you stand?"

Torm shrugged. "I'm tired, Colonel. I've been fighting him for five years—ever since he started his move for power. He's been working up hatred for Earth, whipping the colonists to the edge of revolt, undermining my power every way he can. He thinks the colony could win such a revolt. I know they can't." He looked straight at the Colonel, and his face was white. "There is only one way to reinstate this colony in Earth society as a unit with full rights and privileges—only one way short of violence. And that way is to work together, my people and your people, in mutual trust. But to me, you're an Earthman, and I don't believe a word you say, not one. And I won't, until you give me some reason to. I've been kicked by Earthmen once too often. I'm not going to be kicked again."

Colonel Benedict took a deep breath. "Well, we can discuss this at length later. It looks to me as if you'd better turn Cortell over before we do anything."

"Cortell will be accused and tried in the Titan colony, by a jury of Titan colonists. Not on the Earth ship, and not back on Earth—" The colony leader's voice was cut off by a commotion on the stairs. There was a scuffle of feet, and two burly miners appeared, half-dragging a third man between them. They marched the man across the floor to the desk, then released him, and stood nearby, grimly. "He didn't want to come, Anson," one of the men said sourly. "Didn't seem to think he wanted to see you."

The captive glared at them, then turned his sharp little eyes to Anson Torm. He was a man of medium height, thin and wiry, and he stood like a cornered wildcat, his brown hair disheveled, thin lips drawn back over sharp yellow teeth. When he spoke, his voice was nasal, and hissed through his teeth, as though he were out of breath. "You'll be sorry for this, Torm—you have no warrant to drag me around like this—"

Tom sat back in the chair and blinked up at the man. "There was a land mine in Carter's gorge," he said, his rich bass voice almost conversational. "It wasn't there when the half-track went out to the ship. It *was* there when it came back."

A nasty grin spread over John Cortell's face. "A pity

it didn't get you and these Earth dogs you call your friends—"

Torm rose slowly from the desk, his eyes blazing, and slapped Cortell sharply across the mouth. "It did get my son," he grated. "And these Earth dogs are no more friends of mine than yours. But if they're harmed, the whole colony will suffer—"

Cortell rubbed his mouth, glaring at Torm. "What do you want with me?"

"You and your men laid the mine."

"Really? You have proof of that, of course?"

"Where were you when the half-track left for the ship this afternoon?"

"I was in Smogi's having a drink and waiting for my shift to come due." The grin returned to Cortell's face. "Any more questions? Or are you ready to go back to selling out the colony to these toads?"

Slowly Torm sat back in his chair. His whole body was shaking almost uncontrollably. He found a small printed form in one of the desk drawers, laid it on the table, and started to write. "You're under arrest, John," he said softly. "For attempted murder and treason against the colony. You'll be held for trial, and exportation to Earth if you're convicted." He nodded to the guards. "Take him to his quarters, and post a double guard. There'll be a hearing in public tomorrow. And *no visitors*—"

John Cortell's face went white with rage, and he flew at Torm, slamming his fist down on the desk top. "You don't have proof," he screamed. "You can't prove a thing against me, and when you get through, *see* how long you last as leader of this colony! *Just wait!*" Cortell turned and stalked for the door, with the guards on his heels.

Torm turned to the Colonel, still vibrating with anger. "And as for you, Colonel, I think you'd better start facing facts for a change, you and your Earth people. I'm fighting a battle here to keep a *real* fire from starting in this

67

colony, but I'm losing it. I can't fight it by myself much longer."

Colonel Benedict's eyes were cold. "I have only one job here—to make certain that the supply of ruthenium for Earth is not jeopardized. I'm afraid I'm not much interested in your petty internal struggles for power. They don't interest me except where they affect the supply from the mines."

"Then you won't co-operate with me?"

"Before I can do anything, I need to see the whole picture here in the colony," the Colonel snapped. "So far, an attack has been made on my life and that of my son, and I'm afraid that I can't trust you, either, Mr. Torm. Not with the record you have behind you on this colony. I'm afraid the problems here will have to be settled on Earth terms, regardless of how the colony feels." He turned to Tuck, and took a deep breath. "Right now, I think we'd better see to getting settled in quarters."

Torm stared at them for a long moment, and for the briefest second Tuck thought he saw a light of weary desperation in the big man's eyes. Then finally he stood up, hardly looking at the Colonel and Tuck, and silently led them toward the stairs.

Chapter 7

REVOLT!

Tuck AWOKE with a jerk in the semidarkness of the little
room. He sat up sharply, the whisper of a very unpleasant
dream still drifting in his mind. For a moment of panic
he wondered where he was; then he saw the crude gray
concrete wall curved in over the bed at a sharp angle,
and the brightly painted canvas ceiling of the Torms'
cabin. He stood up in the cold, uneven floor, and felt
every joint in his body scream in protest. He whacked
the rough sleeping pallet with his fist, then wrung his
hand until the pain went away. This was a bed? A hori-
zontal board covered by a lumpy plastic-covered mattress
which couldn't have been an inch thick anywhere! Tuck
groaned, and reached for his clothes, glancing over at
his father's sleeping place. It was empty; the Colonel
must have slept even worse than he had! And yet, there
was an edge of worry that nibbled at Tuck's mind, and
he started rapidly to dress.

Details of the previous evening began to return. There
was the conference with Anson Torm the night before
—and there was the prisoner. Tuck's gloom deepened.
There was a man to watch out for! His mind's eye held
a sharp picture of the twisted, bitter face of John Cortell
as he had strode away with a guard on either side. Both
the Colonel and Torm had been angry at the end of
that meeting, so angry that they barely had spoken on
the way from the meeting room. Tuck recalled his own
feeling of futility and helplessness as he had followed
the two men down the rough road to the small, hut-
like cabin that Torm called his home. It was wrong—

everything was wrong. From the first meeting with Torm something had been awry, some aura of deadly suspicion in the air, yet think as he would, Tuck could not pinpoint it. Torm had shown them their room, and then had left them to their own devices while he went to meet his wife at the infirmary, and to see David.

"But Dad, you didn't even *listen* to him," Tuck had protested as he and his father started unpacking their bag. "I know that we have to be careful, but he was telling the truth, Dad—"

The Colonel sat down, head in his hand. "I wish I could believe that, but I just can't."

"But can't you meet him halfway?"

"There's too much at stake to meet them halfway, son. You heard what Torm said tonight."

Tuck nodded eagerly. "Yes, I did—and if it's true, it makes things add up. The rumors, the ambush in the gorge—"

"How about the bomb in the letter? How about the smuggled supplies? No, there are too many things that *don't* add up."

Tuck sobered. "It's just wrong, somehow. There's something wrong, something we don't know."

"I know. But just suppose the colony *is* planning a revolt, open warfare, real trouble. And then, before they're fully prepared, they get word that we are coming out to investigate. They have agents back on Earth, agents who have been arranging the smuggled shipments for years. Suppose they made a desperate attempt on my life, before I even left Earth—"

"Well, somebody did. But it didn't work."

The Colonel's face hardened. "It *would* have worked. It was a chance in a million that you happened to be home and detect the letter. But you were, so we arrive here. And what happens? Torm appears at the ship, and spends two hours stalling me with denials and accusations. Suppose they need time—maybe just a day or so more to prepare themselves completely for a revolt.

Suppose it's essential to keep us calmed down, out of their hair. What do they do? They carefully stage an ambush, to throw suspicion away from Torm onto a scapegoat. So then, according to the little scenario they've prepared, I'm supposed to confide in Torm, trust him implicitly, tell him everything he wants to know, and they throw the scapegoat in jail so it looks like the trouble is under control, and everything is just rosy—until the rest of the colony has time to finish preparations. And then, boom! Just like that." The Colonel looked up at his son, a twinkle in his eyes. "They're clever, Tuck. They've got the scenario all planned out just perfectly. Only your old man isn't going along with the scenario quite as it was planned—"

"You—you really think this has just been an elaborate cover-up?"

The Colonel shrugged. "I don't know. We're dealing with desperate men."

"You think Anson Torm could be a party to a scheme of that sort?" Tuck stared at his father.

The Colonel stood up, slowly. "You like the man, don't you?"

Tuck's eyes dropped. "I know. I shouldn't, I suppose. It—it doesn't seem right. But I can't help it."

"Well, I'll tell you a little secret, son." The Colonel's eyes were sad. "I like him, too. And that's what's going to be toughest of all. Because I think he's lying in his teeth, and I just don't dare take a chance that he isn't."

They had finished unpacking then, and when the Torms returned there was little conversation. Tuck had not realized how extremely hungry he was, and he watched Mrs. Torm silently from the corner as she prepared the simple meal, and set it down on the table for them. She was a small, quiet woman, looking far older than her years, her face creased with anxiety, and she watched the men with sad, weary eyes, as they ate in silence. Twice she tried unsuccessfully to start pleasant conversation, only to see it dwindle. Finally she said, "I

71

know that there was trouble on the way here, Colonel, and I'm sorry. But I will not have fighting and bitterness carried into my house. There's enough of that in the streets and mines. I want love and friendship in my house." She smiled suddenly, looking years younger. "We have visitors from Earth so seldom. Perhaps you could tell us how things are—back on Earth."

It had been easier, after that. Tuck had joined his father in an account of the new things that had happened back home. The meal was plain, but prepared by an expert hand, and they found the atmosphere in the house at the end of the meal quite different than before the meal. Finally the Colonel brought out his pipe and filled it, then offered the pouch to Anson. The old man's eyes lighted, and he went to a cabinet against the wall, hug deep on a shelf, and came out with an old, old pipe, cracked and blackened with age. "My father's," he said, as he filled it. "Tobacco doesn't come to us very often— there's little room for it on the cargo ships."

The Colonel turned to Mrs. Torm. "And David? How is the boy?"

"He was resting when we saw him. The doctor said there waren't any broken bones or concussion. It just shook him up, but he'll have to stay there a few days, just to make sure—"

Tuck sighed, almost audibly, making a mental note to inquire the way to the infirmary first thing next morning. They had talked on about Earth until very late; then Tuck and his father had retired to their cubicle, set back from the main room of the hut and closed off with a coarse blanket.

"Sorry we can't give you more privacy, but walls are expensive to build," Torm had said apologetically. "Someday we'll have real houses here, I hope. For the time being, I guess you'll be tired enough to sleep."

And now, as Tuck put on his shoes, he wished he had been. Instead of sleeping, he had tossed and turned, his mind spinning over the previous day's events. His father and Torm hadn't spoken of the affairs of the colony all evening, and had seemed almost to be warming toward each other. Yet Tuck couldn't erase his father's words from his mind. *They are clever men, desperate men, and this may just be part of their plan.* For hours he had turned the situation over in his mind, and then had sunk into an uneasy sleep, no closer to the answer than before—

Once dressed, he pushed back the blanket and strode into the main room. The pale morning light was streaming in the open door, and Mrs. Torm was busy in the far end of the room that served as a kitchen. She smiled and nodded to a table. "You're deserted. Your father and Anson left just after daybreak. They're going to tour the mines and check the production schedules today—"

"But they're up so early!"

"You'll have to get used to the short nights—you slept eight hours, and our nights are only six hours long." She set Tuck's breakfast plate down before him. "You'll find it getting dark long before you expect it, too, until you get accustomed to it. The days are shorter." She poured out the milk concentrate and dried, pressed bacon in front of him. The food had a strange look; Tuck tasted it hesitantly, then tore into it like a hungry bear. It seemed like the most delicious breakfast he had ever eaten.

Mrs. Torm left before he had finished, brushing her hair back from her tired face. She explained that she was responsible for the trading post store three days out of six. Tuck finished breakfast slowly, taking in every detail of the rude cabin that he had missed in his weariness the night before. Once again he was struck by the simplicity, the absence of any of the little decorations and refinements that were to be found in every college dormitory room, or every apartment at home. At the far end of the room hung the only picture in the whole place—a gray, faded photograph of a large, strong-faced man, bearing a striking resemblance to Anson Torm, yet even older, with a flowing beard and a fine wide forehead.

Probably David's grandfather, he thought—also a leader of the mining colony years before. And how about David's great-grandfather? Also a leader? Probably. There seemed to be some sort of family succession. That would mean that sometime David might be in line for leadership here. Tuck stared at the picture for a long time. What about the great-great-grandfather? A convict? A murderer? One of the original miners, sent out here to the prison colony, back while Earth was still powered exclusively by atomics? Possibly. There was no way to tell, short of asking, and it struck Tuck that that was hardly the proper sort of question to ask.

"Isn't this a little late to be rolling out of the sack?" The voice boomed from the doorway, and Tuck dropped his fork with a clatter. With a roar of laughter, David Torm was in the room, hands on his hips, grinning broadly at Tuck. "I always heard you folks on Earth were late sleepers—"

Tuck reddened and picked up his fork again, feeling foolish for his sudden start. "I wouldn't say that. You just run a short day out here." He stared at the blond-haired youth. David was even huskier than Tuck had remembered, a powerfully built lad who was never still, always moving. There was a solidity about him that Tuck, with his slender, wiry build, couldn't help but envy. David would be a good friend to have around in a free-for-all, and an unpleasant foe indeed. "I thought you were dying," Tuck said, his eyes twinkling. "Who let you out?"

David chuckled, and started preparing some breakfast with an amazing clatter of pans. "Leetle Davey let himself out. Through the roof. You'd think I'd broken every bone in my body—"

"Ah, well," said Tuck. "They'll just come and drag you back again—"

"They'll need a half-track to do it!"

There was a flicker of concern in Tuck's eyes. "All joking aside—are you sure you feel all right?"

David grinned. "Now I ask you—what kind of pilot would I be if I couldn't crash land a little crate like the *Snooper* without getting hurt? I ask you."

"Well, you were slightly unconscious, no matter what. You scared your father out of ten years."

David shrugged his broad shoulders good-naturedly, and sank down to breakfast. "I've been doing that ever since I learned to walk. Dad's used to it by now. Anyway, there wasn't anything else to do."

"Then you knew there was a trap?"

David shrugged. "It looked like a good bet. I heard that Cortell had something up his sleeve, and it looked to me like a perfect setup for him to wing dad and you folks at the same time—so I just kept you company on the way back." His blue eyes caught Tuck's and held them gravely. "You should have let me talk to dad, back there on the ship. He could have taken a different route back to the colony."

Tuck reddened. "I know. I'm sorry—really I am. I thought you were spying or something—maybe planning to blow us up yourself—"

David threw back his head and roared. "What, and miss a chance to show off the *Snooper?* Everybody thinks it's a big joke around here—Davey's Coffin, they call it."

"Where did it come from?"

"Just an old junk lifeboat that was lying around the colony."

"You fixed it up yourself?"

"Sure. Rebuilt the engine completely. Only jet engine in the Solar System that will fly in Titan atmosphere and nowhere else!"

"What do you do to it?" Tuck felt excitement stir.

David grinned. "Trade secret. Just modified the motor a little, that's all. Everyone said it'd never take off. They just didn't know leetle Davey." He tossed the metal dishes in the sink. "Don't say anything to mother—but I think we can get permission from dad to go out and

75

try to fix up the *Snooper* tomorrow—if you'd want to give me a hand."

"You mean try to make it go again?" Tuck looked dubious. "Do you think it's possible?"

"Won't hurt to try. You ever play around with rocket motors?"

Tuck chuckled. "I've taken so many jet scooters apart and made them go that I could do it in my sleep."

"Good! Maybe between us we can dig it out. But we'll have to wait until dad gets used to my being up and around. He's slow sometimes. Want to take a look around the colony, for the time being?"

"Say, that would be great. I was noticing the big beehive affair in the center of the dome—what is it?" Tuck pulled on his jacket, and stepped out into the street with the other youth, warming to him as they talked. Could a person like that actually be born and grow up in a colony of thieves and murderers? It seemed incredible. They started across the street and up a narrow lane between the cabins toward the odd-looking building. "That's a crude-ore refinery," David was saying. "Can't ship crude ore back to Earth—they haven't got enough ships to carry it. They only get a few grams of pure metal from a ton of ore. and you know about tonnage and pay loads. But we don't have enough power to completely refine the ore, here in the colony, so we split the job halfway. That beehive is the main refining oven, where we break the metal away from the largest bulk of rock." He pointed to the thick metal pipe that led from the building down into the ground. "That pipe carries the slag out about three miles from the colony, where there's a big gorge. We just dump it there. When the gorge gets filled, we'll run it to another gorge. That's one thing about this place —there's plenty of waste space around."

Tuck shook his head as they walked along the rough street.

"I've been thinking," he said. "I don't see how you live out here."

76

"We're used to it. You probably wouldn't last six weeks—you've had it too soft back on Earth. We do what we can to make a little Earth to live in—even if it doesn't seem much like Earth—"

Tuck's eyes were filled with wonder, as they walked. The colony seemed roughly similar to the picture he had in his mind of the old colonial towns in the "wild west" he had loved to read about when he was younger —except that these cabins were made of black rock hewn from the cliffs, and the dust in the road was coal black, and instead of a hot western sun, there was a dull, cold, yellow sun, and the much bigger, brighter planet Saturn giving luster to the landscape. Here and there was a small half-track sitting in the road near a cabin—a far cry from the horses of the days gone by—but there were the same men, with the craggy, weather-beaten faces and powerfully muscled arms, the same plainly dressed women, cheerful even in such gloomy surroundings as these. Occasionally they passed boys and girls their own age, who nodded to David in greeting. As the boys trudged along, Tuck's confusion grew and grew. This colony—a strange place, yes, but basically it was just another town. And the people seemed ordinary enough, just like other people. His face must have registered his feelings.

David Torm looked at him, and burst out laughing. "You look like you've swallowed a frog. What's wrong?"

Tuck shook his head. "It's—so different from what I expected—"

There was mischief in David's eyes. "Not even one murder on the street so far, eh? No two-headed monsters—why, we didn't even have our best family daggers out to eat breakfast with—"

Tuck flushed hotly and started to reply, then closed his mouth. "I don't see what's so funny," he said.

"But you're surprised. What did you expect?"

"I—I don't know. But not *this*."

David Torm grinned. "Of course, we're on our good

behavior while you're here. Normally we go around clawing at each other, and gnawing our food uncooked. And every night or so we have war dances and blood orgies, and plot attacks on Earth, and plan the huge massacres we'll have when we get power enough to start a war with Earth—oh, don't look so surprised! I know all about the stories they tell you. They sound a little silly to us, but we know about them—"

Tuck stared at him. "But—everybody on Earth knows those things are true. I've always heard them, since I was a very little boy—I never even *thought* about it— why should I have? If everybody accepted it—"

David's face was heavy with disgust. "Well. I hate to upset all these years of nice careful teaching, but it just isn't true. It's a lie. And probably everything you've ever heard about us is a lie."

"But *why?*"

"Fear. Figure it out for yourself. And then forget what you've been told about us, and give us a break, just once."

Tuck's face was horrified. "But they've done it so *thoroughly—*"

"I know. But they've forgotten one thing. We *are* human beings. And the result is an account of hatred among the colonists that goes four generations deep into our grain. Dad has been trying to cure that hatred before it's too late. But dad can't hold out much longer. If something doesn't stop it, the Big Secret will be out of the bag—" David stopped short. hand to his lips, looking away quickly.

"The Big Secret?"

David squirmed uncomfortably. "Nothing. Just an old colony folk tale about a last-ditch stand against Earthmen, if things ever came to a showdown."

Tuck's eyes widened. "What kind of a showdown?"

But David was no longer paying attention. His eyes were fixed down the road, watching something intently. "Hey!" said Tuck. "I said—"

Quiet!" The word was a whispered command. David

slid back against the wall of the building, motioning Tuck back—

"What's wrong?"

"Take a look—see that man in the green shirt?"

Tuck saw him. He was making his way stealthily along the road, looking to the right and left as he moved, like a cat, out from the protection of one cabin wall, quickly across to the next. He paused at a cabin door, rapped on it, and the boys could see him talking to the man inside, gesticulating rapidly. Then he was on to the cabin across the road—

"Who is it?"

"Johnny Taggart. The man who probably set the mine in Carter's gorge. One of Cortell's first lieutenants. He's supposed to be confined to quarters, just like Cortell—"

"*But what's he doing out?*"

"I don't know. Something's up—"

Several of the colonists were gathering at their doors, whispering, watching as the man hurried along. David touched Tuck's arm. "Come on. There's trouble—I'm sure of it. We'd better find dad and let him know. Follow me."

The boys darted behind the building where they were standing, and then broke into a run into another street, back like the wind towards the barracks building. And then, suddenly, a siren sounded, high and biting in the quiet air of the dome. David's eyes widened. "I told you something was up," he panted. They ran pellmell down a narrow alley-like road, then slowed up, making their way through the excited crowd that was gathered around the trading post. There was a buzz of conversation, and the boys broke through the crowd just as Anson Torm and the Colonel were coming out.

"What's the trouble, Dad?" David panted. "A leak in the tunnels?"

Anson Torm's face was gray. "Worse, I'm afraid. Come on over to the house." The colony leader nodded to Ned

Miller, who started shouting for order, standing up on the porch of the trading post as Torm and the Colonel and the two boys crossed the road to the Torm cabin. "John Cortell's broken prison with his two top men. They're at large somewhere in the colony, and they've got to be found, and fast," Anson Torm said.

"But—why the alarm? The siren—"

"Because the word is around that Cortell is calling a showdown on me, because of the Colonel's presence here. He thinks he's strong enough to get a wholesale revolt organized, and to blow up the mines." Torm's voice was hollow, and his hands were trembling as he sank down in the chair by the table. "And I'm just afraid he might be able to swing it—"

Chapter 8

"THAT MAN IS DANGEROUS—"

THERE WERE a dozen men gathered in the underground meeting room when Anson Torm and the Colonel arrived there with the two boys. Many of the men were blackened with the thick dust of the mining tunnels; apparently they had stopped work and come up to the hall as soon as the alarm had sounded. Torm nodded to the group, and sat down at the desk, his face drawn and white. "Now, then. Exactly what happened?" He looked at one of the men.

"Cortell's a magician," the man growled. "I can't tell you what happened, Anson. I don't know. I was on duty with Klane, guarding him in his cabin. I was inside and Klane was outside. Nobody had been near him, and he'd been at me all night with his abuse—he's got a nasty tongue—and then, out of a clear blue sky, he had a gun on me. Forced me to distract Klane's attention outside, and two others piled on him—and then they were gone."

"He didn't have a gun when you searched him before?"

"No, sir. He was clean as a whistle."

Torm's cold blue eyes flashed to another man. "The arsenal," he said. "Did you check the arsenal?"

"Just got back. It's been broken into."

"How many guns gone?"

"Less than a dozen."

"Good. Get the rest of the guns, and lock them in the safe down here, so there won't be any more stolen. If we can keep weapons out of their hands—"

The arsenal guard was shaking his head. "You'd better let me have a couple of men to go with me," he said dubiously.

Torm frowned. "What's wrong?"

"There's a nasty crowd at the arsenal. Rog Strang's with them. They aren't doing anything, but they're with Cortell all the way. They could put up a fight—"

Torm stripped a small, unpleasant-looking automatic from his belt and tossed it to the guard. "Take Klane and Simpson with you, and *get those guns down here*."

Torm turned back to the group of men. "Now, then, for Cortell himself. There are plenty of people in this colony who will help him if they can. But Cortell and his boys can't get out of the colony without our knowing it—we've got all the pressure locks under guard. So we can be pretty sure they're in here, somewhere. Jack, you take your group and comb everything topside—every cabin, every building. Don't miss anything—"

"Anson, the people won't take it." The man was a huge, black-faced miner. "He's got support, and they'll fight us down."

"Those that are with us will help—recruit them as you go along. As for the others—" he glanced at the miner. "That's why you have the gun. Cortell is under arrest for attempted murder, and if they're hiding him, they're accomplices. Now get going." The group of men shuffled out. Torm leaned back and motioned to the man who had just come down the stairs. "What do you think, Ned?"

"I don't know." Ned Miller's face was tired. "Johnny Taggart has been contacting all his supporters—"

"Oh, I know it—it's all over the colony. And they know their propaganda methods." Torm shot Colonel Benedict a black look. "The question is, what now? What's he going to do?"

Ned scowled. "If he can't get more guns, he's blocked for a while. But there's no hope of finding him, if he doesn't want to be found. He won't be hiding above ground—"

"I know that. But we've got to be sure, and get the folks on his side worried about helping him. Jack and the gang will take care of that."

The dirty little man rubbed his stubbled chin and nodded. "So he's down in the mines somewhere, with guns enough to blockade himself in even if we found him." He also glanced at Colonel Benedict, and suddenly dropped his voice to a whisper.

Torm began shaking his head vigorously. "He couldn't do that. Not yet—the stockpile just isn't big enough. That's what I don't like about this—he *couldn't* be ready at this point. Unless he's changed his plans, somehow. He just wouldn't dare try it—"

For the first time Colonel Benedict stood up, turned to Torm. "I take it you don't expect to find this madman."

Torm looked up with cold blue eyes. "We don't stand a chance in a million, thanks to you. Cortell's support is growing every minute. He's got over a third of the colony on his side now—and with that he can hide where he likes, and he'll never be found."

The Colonel scowled. "That's very nice," he said sourly. "And just what is it that Cortell wouldn't try?"

Torm's eyes narrowed. "He can't do anything—or at least he won't, as long as we can keep weapons out of his hands."

"These mining tunnels—they go for miles back underground, don't they?"

Torm's eyes flickered. "That's right."

"And how many tunnels are there?"

"Dozens. There are three or four hundred miles of tunnel going out of the colony, one place or another—"

"Then what's to prevent Cortell from holing himself up in one of the tunnels with his friends, and blowing the entire colony to kingdom come?"

"Nothing could prevent it, if Cortell wanted to do it. It would be very simple. There's methane outside on the planet's surface. It would be a simple matter to break through someplace in the tunnel and let methane into the colony—he could do it in a dozen places, and we wouldn't have a chance of stopping him. And then when it got to a critical mixture, just a single spark, a single lit match, and the colony would go off like an atom bomb." Torm's eyes met the Colonel's defiantly. "Anyone in this colony could have done that, years ago—but we haven't. And Cortell won't do it, either. Not now."

"Why not?"

"What would it accomplish? There he'd be, and as soon as his supplies gave out, or his oxygen, he'd be as dead as we were."

Colonel Benedict leaned over the desk, staring straight at the colony leader. "But for years and years supplies have been coming in here, smuggled supplies, above the colony's quota, Anson. Food, plants, equipment, tools—everything." His eyes blazed. "I think it's time for you to do some talking. I'm tired of this runaround. I want to know where those supplies have gone, and what Cortell plans to do with them. I want to know who's behind the smuggling that's been going on, and *why* it's been going on." The Colonel's knuckles tightened on his chair. "A criminal is at large in the colony, and you sit quietly by and say, 'Oh, he won't hurt anybody, he won't do any damage, let him be.' All right, if Cortell is not able to put his plans for revolt in action now, I want to know why not."

Torm spread his hands. "He just won't. He can't."

"*Then what's blocking him?*"

Anson Torm's face was set. He didn't answer.

"I want the truth, Torm. What are his plans? What's blocking him?"

"I can't tell you—" He broke off as a group of men came tumbling down the stairs into the meeting room, angry-faced men, talking rapidly among themselves.

84

They gathered in a group, still muttering angrily and looking darkly at Anson Torm when a tall, thin man walked up to Torm, hands on his belt. "What's the idea of sending men up with guns to break out the arsenal?" The man's anger was barely controlled as he glared down at the colony leader.

Anson Torm looked up calmly. Then he nodded to the Colonel. "This is Colonel Benedict, of Earth Security. Colonel, meet Rog Strang."

The man called Strang glared at the Colonel for a moment, and then spat on the floor. "I didn't come to talk to this scum. I came to talk to you. Your men are cleaning out the arsenal. What's the idea?"

"I ordered them to. There were guns stolen from it last night, as you probably know well enough. Cortell is at large, as you also know quite well. And as long as I'm leader of this colony, Cortell's not going to get any more guns."

Strang sneered. "Maybe you're not going to be leader for so long. The people want you to lay off Cortell. He's the only one who's talking sense around here, and he says the time has come to quit taking it lying down from Earth Security. What do you say to that, Anson?"

"Noble sentiments, indeed. Only thing is, Cortell talks too much." Torm's pale eyes caught the other man's. "Any more foolish questions, Strang, or are you ready to take your friends back out of here?"

The man's hand was trembling angrily. "The people won't take it much longer. They want Cortell cleared."

"*Some* of the people, you mean. There's been no convention and no election, to my knowledge. Until there is, I'm still in charge here, and my warrant for Cortell stands."

The man turned on his heel and started to go, then turned once again to Torm, his eyes wild. "There's nasty talk around, Anson. Talk about *you* being the traitor, selling out to these Earth dogs. What are they offering you, Anson? Safe passage back to Earth? A nice place to live for the rest of your life, with hot and cold running water—?"

"*Get out of here, Strang*." Torm's voice sounded rusty, and his hands gripped his chair until his knuckles were white. As the group went up the stairs, he turned to the Colonel. "I can't sit here and talk any longer—I've got to get a search of the tunnels organized. Cortell won't do anything just now—I can't tell you why, you'll just have to take my word for it. But I warn you, Colonel—this is a fight to the finish, this time. If Cortell can win the colony to his side, it'll all be over. The people hate you and Earth with four generations of hate, and Cortell is playing that hate for all it's worth. It's up to you, now. If you're ready to trust me and make a square and honorable deal with the Titan colonists, there may be time to save things. But time is running out—" He stood up and walked for the stairs with a group of his men around him. "We'll have to split up the tunnels among us," he was saying as they went up the stairs. "And we'll have to go slow . . ."

Tuck and David sat side by side, watching the Colonel. He sat for a long time in silence, his face looking older than Tuck had ever seen it before. Then he slammed his fist down on the table with a groan. "The fool!" he grated. "The stubborn fool! Security will never accept a deal. What does he think he can get with this kind of blackmail? All Security wants is to have the trouble stopped and production continued smoothly—and thanks to him we're in the middle of the worst trouble there's been in years."

"Dad—" Tuck looked up at his father. "Dad, Torm is right. You have to trust him."

"How can I trust him?" the Colonel exploded. "Why won't he come clean? Why won't he tell me what Cortell has up his sleeve?"

"I don't know—but does it really matter? I mean, if you could take Torm at his word, and start negotiating—"

"But how could I ever sell Security on it? How could I tell them to trust the colonists when I'm not even convinced myself?" He shook his head tiredly, and stood up. "No, it won't work. There'll be no deals until Torm lays the truth on the line. Until then, he's just another colonist rebel, I'm afraid." He started for the stairs.

"Dad, what are you going to do?"

"I don't know. Wait, I guess. I just don't know." His shoulders sagged as he walked up the stairs.

Tuck turned to David Torm, and made a hopeless gesture. "They can't see each other. Every time they talk, they get farther apart. Dad is so sure that anything anybody does out here is aimed against Earth that he won't even listen."

David's eyes were wide. "But he's *got* to see," he said excitedly. "Does he realize what's happening? That man Cortell is dangerous, and he's ruthless."

Tuck nodded. "Yes—but your father isn't coming halfway, either—"

"I know it." David flopped dejectedly down in the chair. "Why are people so stupid? Dad doesn't hate Earthmen—he just distrusts them. He's seen too many back-stabbing tricks to trust them. But Cortell isn't made like dad. He's all hate—he lives on it. He hates Earth and everything about Earth."

Tuck looked at David. "Yet he's in contact with people on Earth. That's one reason dad won't co-operate. They tried to kill him, back home, before he even started out here." David's eyes widened as Tuck told him about the Murexide bomb in the strange letter. When Tuck was finished, David whistled softly.

"My father doesn't know about that, does he?"

"No."

The lad paced back and forth like a caged animal. "It must have been Cortell who arranged it. Yet, I don't see—" He scowled and paced some more. "There must be something *we* can do—" He grinned at the Earth boy. "At least we can talk without going for each other's throats. And Cortell has got to be stopped. He can carry the whole colony to suicide if he wins—"

Tuck turned slowly to David. "*Suicide?* What do you mean?"

The leader's son looked at Tuck queerly, a sudden light of excitement on his broad face. "Listen," he said. "I—I think I know an answer."

"Answer?"

"To the whole problem—a way out, a way to stop Cortell, and to make dad and the Colonel see things eye to eye—" He looked straight at Tuck. "I'd have to count on you completely not to spill it too early—"

"You can count on it."

"And—I hate to say it, but you'll have to trust me."

Tuck hesitated just a moment. Then he looked up at David and nodded.

"Then come on!" David was on his feet, half running for the stairs. "I've got something to tell you, but I think we'd better get away from the colony before we talk. Dad would break my neck if he caught on before we had a chance—"

"But where can we go?"

"They're busy hunting for Cortell—they'd be glad to have us out of the way if some shooting starts. Let's go out and see what shape the *Snooper* is in—right now!"

The guard at the gate was not co-operative. Orders were, nobody went out. For a while prospects looked gloomy, but as Tuck had seen before, his companion had a gift of gab. In two minutes the guard was so completely confused with the barrage released upon him that he broke down, muttering darkly about little wise guys and the penalties for disobeying orders, and opened the inner lock. With a grin from ear to ear David slammed down the top on the half-track. Five minutes later they were rolling through the lock into the open atmosphere of Titan, heading away from the colony at top speed, in the direction of the wreck of the *Snooper*.

Chapter 9

THE BIG SECRET

THE TRIP out was wild. There was nothing in David Torm's nature to allow for caution and comfort; he rode the half-track like a bucking bronco, whirling the steering bar with gleeful abandon as the car tossed and tumbled across the uneven rocky terrain away from the dome of the colony. The soft pillow wheels absorbed some of the shock, but Tuck strapped himself down and clung to the safety bar for dear life, as they lurched from side to side. David whistled cheerfully to himself above the engine's tortured roar, peering ahead at the path, swerving wildly to the left or right as boulders too large to climb over came into the path of the vehicle. Up in the sky the sun was just as the meridian, and little swirls of snow, white and powdery, spun up in the dead, still atmosphere as the half-track plunged along like some strange, half-possessed monster.

David swerved suddenly, as the wheels of the 'track slipped into an almost invisible crevice, and the machine gave a bone-crushing lurch to one side.

"Yi!" said Tuck, feeling slightly green.

"Yi, yourself," said David, throwing the car into reverse and jerking loose from the crevice. The motor responded with a grating of gears, and started climbing again. "Me and this 'track, we understand each other."

"So it seems," said Tuck, weakly. "You try to kill it, and it tries to kill you. Nice and cozy—"

David grinned. "Keep your eyes open now. Seems to me the *Snooper* should be a couple of miles over to the left of the main road to the rocket landing—isn't that right? I hit pretty fast after the explosion, but I came in nearly three point, so I must have had a couple of miles of skimming."

Tuck shook his head. "It looked to me as if you were barrel rolling all the way."

"Me? Barrel roll? Never!"

"Well, you didn't have much to say about it."

"That's for sure. Felt like somebody came up behind and whacked me with a large stone wall." He braked the machine, and peered out in the strange, gloomy light. "There, now. See the tracks? That must be where dad's 'track came back onto the path after he picked me up." David jerked the steering rod again, and this time the 'track moved sharply to the right, mounted a rocky rise, and tumbled down, jerking from side to side as the caterpillar tracks bit the unfamiliar coarse terrain. Tuck gritted his teeth, and felt his hands clench the gripping bar. "I hope *you* know what you're doing," he growled. "That felt like we were going to roll—"

"So we turn it over—so what? This plastic on the top will take a lot of punishment. There are even fancy jacks in the back to turn it back right side up if it rolls."

Tuck gripped the bar tighter. "Do they roll very often?"

David laughed. "Don't get excited. It doesn't happen often. But if you get caught after dark, the emergency lights make the crevices look just like more rock, and then anything can happen. I spent a week in the bottom of a crevice once, until they came and found me. Why, there was one time—" he jerked the wheel hard—"when I ran one of these things right up on top of a great big clordelkus before he decided that now was the time to go somewhere else—"

Tuck grinned, remembering his first scare at seeing one of those. The 'track was following a faint path in the snow left by the 'track before them, and far ahead and to the right Tuck could see the gorge, or what remained of it, where the explosion had occurred. The sight drew his mind back to the things that had happened since the Earth ship had landed—back to the impending crisis at the colony. He watched the leader's son, thoughtfully, as the lad fought the steering bar of the half-track. Odd that he should be sitting here, perfectly confident in the friendship he felt growing between them—a friendship that was ridiculous by all the standards Tuck had ever known. He wondered if David had even thought of the strangeness of their friendship under these circumstances. Probably not. And yet David was ready to take him into his confidence, with little more than his word for security. Quite suddenly, Tuck felt a pang of shame for his suspiciousness, for his father's stubbornness—above all, for his own reluctance to admit to himself that Earth Security's position might, conceivably, be wrong. This was so futile, so needless—

And yet there was John Cortell. The thought sent a chill down Tuck's spine. "It would be nice if they had caught Cortell by the time we get back," he said wistfully. "That would solve a lot of problems."

David snorted. "Well, they won't, so don't figure on it. They aren't going to get near to catching Cortell—and dad knows it."

"How can you be so sure? It seems to me there's just so much of the colony to search."

David nodded. "That's right. But it's deceptive. We're right over a part of the colony now, even though we're three miles away from the dome."

Tuck glanced down at the black rock path involuntarily. "Tunnel?"

David nodded. "They go out in all directions—a regular maze. Down about forty feet deep, and even then we have trouble with cave-ins and quakes and landslides." He hung onto the bar precariously with one hand, pointing to a long outcropping of rock to the right. "See that? That's a rich vein—goes out almost twenty miles. They mine it and run the ore back to the refinery on railroad tracks laid in there. Got a whole little supply unit in the mining area—whoops!" The car lurched and dropped about six feet, jarring their very bones. David spun the steering bar and went right on talking as Tuck picked himself up from the dashboard. "The tunnels are all interconnecting, everywhere. Get somebody in there who doesn't know their plan, and he could starve to death trying to get out. But Cortell—"

"I suppose he knows every tunnel," Tuck remarked glumly.

"Like the back of his hand. He could hide there till doomsday, and nobody'd ever find him. And he's got plenty of friends to help him, too. If a search party comes close to him, Cortell gets the word, and moves somewhere else. Oh, he's a clever one—"

Tuck blinked. "Then it seems to me that all this hunting is rather silly."

David grinned. "Good boy. Comes the dawn." He jerked the wheel sharply, avoiding a huge black outcropping, and plunged the half-track down into a shallow gully with high, overhanging crags on both sides.

"But why is your father pretending—"

"Not pretending. He's hunting. But he needs time— he needs time worse than anything. And he needs to keep the men that are on his side good and busy until he can get your father to see things the colony's way." He looked soberly at Tuck. "Want to know the facts of life?"

"Tell me the facts of life."

"Okay, Bub. Fact number one: your father is going to have to give in and go along with dad. If he doesn't, the fat's in the fire. Cortell will have enough time to put his plans into action—"

"But what's holding him up now?"

"Aha! He can't do what he wants to do now, and dad knows it. That's fact number two—but I'm coming to that. Don't interrupt. Fact number three: if dad can keep his own boys with him long enough to make a settlement with your father, he can cut the floor right out from under Cortell. And that's where my little scheme comes in—"

Tuck scowled, gripping the bar tightly as the 'track climbed back out of a gully, slowly, painfully, like a roller coaster climbing up for its first big plunge. "But I still don't see what Cortell is planning to do—"

David slowed the 'track down suddenly, and braked it, snapping the motor off. He stretched his arms for a moment, then turned to Tuck. "Think about it a minute," he said. "The whole picture. They teach you logic and data evaluation in your Earth schools. Look at the facts. An angry crowd of people out here, being walked all over for years and years. I don't care whether you believe that or not—I *know* it's true. They've been kicked for years. No hope of changes—things getting worse and worse for them as the ruthenium gets more and more important for Earth No end in sight—are you with me?"

Tuck nodded. "So far."

"Good. Then the smuggled supplies coming out here —oh, they've been coming out here, all right. And they've been smuggled, too. Then your father gets appointed to come out here. Why? To trace down smuggled supplies. And what happens? They try to clip him—"

"*Who* tries to clip him?"

David held up his hand. "Just hold on a minute. *Somebody*—it doesn't matter who. But the attempt backfires, you and your father come out here anyway—tracing down the supplies. And then Cortell moves and threatens *something*—and my father won't tell your father what." David looked at Tuck narrowly. "You're the one that's been to school. Now I ask you—what does all that add up to?"

Tuck chewed his lip. "Cortell is desperate that the smuggled supplies not be found," he said suddenly. He looked at David. "*And so is your father.*"

"Huzzah," said David.

93

"Why—this begins to make sense!" Tuck's excitement rose. "You even made a slip about it, that first morning in the colony—"

David nodded. "The Big Secret," he said.

"Something both Cortell and your father know about, and your father doesn't dare tell dad about!"

David nodded glumly. "It's a plan," he said, his voice almost a whisper. "There's been a plan for a long, long time, here in the colony. My father would break my neck if he ever knew I'd told you this. It's been so well guarded that there aren't more than six or seven in the colony now who know exactly *what* the plan is, or how it's supposed to work—"

"But what *is* it?"

David shook his head. "I don't know. I mean, I don't know *specifically*—" He saw Tuck's face, and shook his head again. "No, no—I'm not holding out on you. I honestly *don't* know. Hardly anybody knows, although everybody has his pet theory. It got started over a hundred years ago, and everyone in the colony has helped with it, one way or another—but only a few chosen ones have known exactly what it is."

"But when did it start?"

David spread his hands. "Years ago. Back in the very earliest days, when our leaders began to see what Earth Security was trying to do. Oh, they were bitter in those days—there were strikes, and fighting and protest—it was really gay. But whenever there was an outbreak, Security just cut off supplies and let the colony starve for a while. It worked fine—but even a hundred years ago the colony could see what was coming. Titan was going to end up a slave colony, with no rights of any kind, and no place to go in the whole Solar System. It was like the old horror story I read once about the guy being walled up in a cellar brick by brick. So the leaders held a council. *Sometime* things would come to a breaking point. They had to make plans for that time, while they could, or the Colony would never be free again. So they came up with the Big Secret."

Tuck frowned. "I don't see how it could work. How could everyone help if nobody knew what it was? Why all the secrecy?"

"Why? With Security watching us like bugs under a glass? It *had* to be secret. It was a big plan, a plan that would take years to prepare. And it was to be a last-ditch retreat for the colonists—maybe a huge, barricaded, carefully hidden underground colony, where the colonists could go and blockade themselves in, and then blow the mines to smithereens, and all Earth's precious ruthenium with it. Oh, it's possible. After all, we're used to living in cramped quarters, we're used to little food, we can even take a lower oxygen concentration for a longer time than you can. They started it, back in the early days, cutting down their rations, saving little bits of food under deepfreeze; they got supporters back on Earth, got them wormed into Security, and started a grand smuggling program to bring out supplies. And once here, the goods were secretly stored, and then passed on to the five or six men who were guarding the Secret. And there were clothes, made out of scraps—clothes to keep 500 people warm, and tools and oxygen—for over a hundred years every oxygen tank that has been used here has been closed down for empty when it was only three-quarters gone. And all this to prepare the Big Secret for action when the time came." David shook his head. "I don't know *what* it is, or *where* it is—it may be carved out of rock a hundred miles straight down in the ground —or somewhere on the other side of the planet."

Tuck stared numbly at the leader's son. "It would be suicide," he whispered. "They'd—they'd be sealing themselves up forever. They could *never* come out! And they'd have every patrol soldier in the Solar System here on Titan, hunting them down—"

David shrugged. "Back in Earth legend, a guy named

Horatio guarded a bridge against a whole army. They could do the same—and they could hold out for years, even if their location were found."

"And after years—then what?"

David nodded unhappily. "That's the big hitch. They could last for twenty, thirty, fifty years—but they'd be dead men, in the long run. That's what dad believes. He thinks the Big Secret, whatever it is, is sure suicide for the colony. That's why he fought against it, tried to slow down its completion as much as he could, for fear the colony would reach the breaking point while there was still a chance of peaceful change and negotiation. But Cortell has been leading his group to believe that the breaking point has passed, that the time has come, that they should start the Big Secret into action right now, whatever it is. Oh, dad is no fool, he *knows* what the Big Secret is—but Cortell has a lot of the colonists believing that dad is a weakling and a traitor, that it's too late ever to establish peace with Earth—"

"But your father is still strong in the colony—"

"He was—until now. He's losing strength fast. A lot of people believed that he *would* be able to negotiate with the Colonel. But the important thing is that the Big Secret just isn't ready to put into operation yet. It's nearly ready, but not quite."

Tuck nodded. "Five hundred people are a lot to take care of—for a long period of time."

"And how! And dad is trying to make the people see that they're choosing suicide if they follow Cortell." The leader's son started the motor again. "Dad doesn't dare spill the whole story to the Colonel, because he thinks the Colonel would clamp down and report it to Security—which he probably would, considering the state he's in. Dad's hogtied. Earthmen and Titan colonists have hated each other for so long that they can't imagine trusting each other. They're from different ends of the Universe."

The half-track started again with a lurch, and reached

the top of the gully, started lumbering down the side. Both boys peered eagerly ahead; then suddenly Tuck let out a shout. "Over to the right—see it?"

David squinted against the sun. "I think—yes! That's it!" The half-track bounced forward with renewed speed as they approached the glinting metal that had been the *Snooper*. At first all they could see was the tail, sticking out from behind an outcropping of rock; then the 'track moved around the rock, and they saw the wreck—

It had skimmed on its belly, ripping off one of its sled tracks, and the sharp rocks had ripped long, curling strips of the underfuselage away from the braces. The nose had burrowed a ten-foot-long ditch, and one of the little stabilizer wings had been ripped almost completely off. But worst of all, the exhaust tube showed a long, crooked split that ran right back its length toward the jet engines—

Tuck felt his heart sink. They would need tools, welding—they'd practically need a machine shop to put the little scooter back into the air. He turned to David, all his excited hopes of exploration on the rugged planet surface dashed into the black rocks just like the *Snooper* itself. "Looks like we're out of luck."

David eyed the wreckage critically. "Hmmm—" he said. "Have to weld the exhaust tube—may even have wrecked the combustion chamber—I don't know. But the thing was in a lot worse shape when I first put it together." He looked at Tuck. "Are you game to try?"

"Well, we can't do it any *harm*—"

"Then come on!" David checked the helmet to his pressure suit, and started to open the half-track top. "Between the two of us, we should be able to get the thing back into shape—maybe it won't take as much work as it looks." He was out of the half-track, moving toward the back of it when Tuck got his suit heater controls readjusted and clambered out, wondering just what they were going to work *with*. And then he saw the whole rear casing of the half-track peel away to reveal a huge tool case, complete with three or four large gas bottles, welding torches, metal siding, and a dozen different types of wiring on neat spools along the top.

It would be work, but there was lots of daylight left, and there were emergency lights on the 'track if they couldn't finish by dark. In a few moments both boys were struggling with the gas bottles, dragging them over toward the *Snooper*, and David was clambering up into the cockpit gleefully, disappearing into the broken fuselage.

But even as he moved toward the little ship, Tuck was mulling over David's words. A secret, a wild, hopeless plan that would destroy Earth's power source, utterly and irreparably. A single word, a flick of the wrist, and everything could be lost. And neither Colonel Benedict nor Anson Torm could cross the barrier of hatred and distrust that had built up between their peoples over the years. Tuck's heart sank gloomily. It was too much to expect. Nobody could cast aside a lifetime of teaching, and trust someone he had been drilled and drilled so carefully to distrust and hate. Not even a fine and wise man like his father could cross a barrier like that. *Nobody* could do it—

He stopped cold in his tracks, and stared at the little ship below him, stared at the suited and helmeted figure now climbing out of the cockpit and waving at him.

Nobody?

He was Tuck Benedict, an Earthman—and that was David Torm, a Titan miner's son and a colonist, a rebel, a traitor, a sneak, a murderer, by everything Tuck had ever been taught—and they were working together for something they both wanted badly—

And they were friends, and they trusted each other—

Suddenly a great weight lifted from Tuck's chest. *Nobody?* He hoisted up the gas bottle and started for the ship as fast as he could go, his heart tearing in his chest, his pulse pounding. *They* were somebody, and somehow, insidiously, without even giving it a thought, they had succeeded in doing the unheard of, the very thing that had never been achieved since the earliest days of the Titan colony. He reached the ship, gasping for breath just as David got to the ground, took the bottle and set it alongside the others. "Not bad up there," he said. "There's a lot of outside tearing, but if we can seal up the cockpit and the engines, it might just work." David grinned at Tuck. "How about it? Ready to start?"

Tuck grinned back, feeling happier than he had ever felt in his life. "Ready? Buddy, we're going to make this wreck run like it never ran before. And when we have it running, you and I have a job to do!"

"You mean—"

"I mean we're going to teach our respective fathers the facts of life, or know the reason why!"

Chapter 10

THE WRECK OF THE SNOOPER

FOR THE NEXT ten minutes the boys inspected the wreckage at close hand. It looked almost hopeless to Tuck, at first, but much of the more obvious damage involved ripped siding, which could be easily replaced. The cockpit was almost intact, except or the long crack in the plastic hood, and the shattered control board. Tuck worked away at the paneling, and finally broke it loose, revealing the masses of wires leading to the pressure, fuel, speed and altitude controls. With a few minutes' work he had straightened or repaired the broken wires, and the panel was replaced, ready for seal-welding.

But the engines were another story. The rear end of the jet was smashed almost closed; a long crack ran clear back to the engine, and a whole section of wiring had been ripped from its moorings. The two started to work, with crowbar and hammer, slowly breaking and wrenching the little ship from its bed of rock, talking very little as they worked. From time to time Tuck stopped to stare at the engine and the wiring that were exposed. They didn't look at all right, for some reason, and the more he looked the more puzzled he became. And then it dawned on him—the whole area where the fuel tanks belonged was filled with large gas bottles painted green, without the familiar insulating pad around them. Tuck looked up at David, hardly believing his eyes. "Say, what kind of engine have you got in this thing?"

David stopped prying at the crowbar long enough to grin. "Ordinary jet combustion chamber. Torm modification."

Tuck looked suspicious. "But those are *oxygen* bottles in there—"

"That's right. That's the Torm modification."

"But what do you use for fuel?"

"Oxygen." David grinned at his friend's consternation, then burst out laughing. "It's really very simple. When the jet is flying, it doesn't take *air* into the intakes, the way you're used to. It couldn't—there isn't any air. It takes *methane* into the air-scoop. So why use a lot of expensive fuel and oxidizer, when all the fuel you could possibly use is free for the asking, all around you?"

"You mean you use atmospheric methane for your fuel?"

"Of course. The pumps just feed in a tiny stream of liquid oxygen from those tanks there into the center of the intake of methane. Makes a funny-looking exhaust —just a pencil-thin flame—but it works, delivers plenty of thrust. And all I have to carry is priming fuel and oxygen—"

Tuck examined the setup excitedly. "You must have been all over the planet with this!"

"It's been handy. Some other guys here in the colony worked with me on it. We taught ourselves mapping and topography from some books my dad has. We've had a lot of fun, just snooping around with it, and we've made our own maps of the topography within a couple hundred square miles of the colony. Better than Security Patrol maps, too." David stood up from the crowbar and started rolling a large green oxygen bottle over toward the damaged jet. "Let me show you another little trick with oxygen," he said.

He had been working for a quarter of an hour, driving a wedge into the opening, gradually forcing the squashed tube open again, revealing a long rip in the heavy metal of the exhaust tube. Now he fished in the small bag of little tools and came out with a bit of metal that looked like a small brass hose nozzle, which he carefully fitted

101

to a long aluminum mesh tube that stretched from the neck of the oxygem bottle.

"What are you going to do?"

"Have to weld, for a while."

"Weld! What do you use for a generator?"

"Oh, I don't mean arc-weld. That isn't necessary, and we've got a better method here." He reached for the control gauge at the top of the green bottle, and brought a small automatic flint up near the nozzle; then he carefully opened the gauge until there was the slightest hiss from the nozzle, and struck a spark. To Tuck's amazement a bright white flame sprang from the nozzle of the nose, giving off a brilliant shower of white snow. The snow scattered and drifted to the ground, for all the world like the snow from a carbon-dioxide fire extinguisher. Tuck stood frozen for a moment, then jumped back, his heart pounding. "Are you crazy? That's *oxygen* in that tank!"

"I know."

"But it's *burning*—won't it explode in this atmosphere?"

"Not as long as I keep the gas flowing from the tank." David began pulling the flaming nozzle down toward the metal of the jet, and started heating the edge of the open tear. "There won't be an explosion as long as there's plenty of room for the burning to take place, and the flame can consume the oxygen as fast as it comes out of the tank. Makes a nice hot flame, too." The lips of the rent were beginning to turn pinkish already. "There's no danger at all of welding with oxygen out here—the real danger of explosion is in a confined space, like a mining tunnel. There, if the tunnel springs a leak somewhere, a lot of methane can squeeze it before anyone realizes it, and any little spark can send up the whole works. It's a real hazard in the tunnels. We even have special detecting equipment to set off an alarm as soon as a leak breaks loose."

"What can they do in the tunnel once the methane gets in?"

David grinned. "Run in circles, scream and shout. Seal off the leak as fast as they can, close off the tunnel from the rest of the colony, and pump for dear life. So far they've been lucky."

He bent over, applying the torch to the hot metal of the jet, as though unwilling to think about such horrible possibilities. The metal was white-hot now; David handed the torch to Tuck, had him hold it nearby, bathing the metal in the stream of white flame, while David began hammering, sending up a shower of sparks. The snow that streamed from the torch formed a little pile on the ground some lit on the hot metal, hissed, and burst into clouds of steam that promptly became snow again as soon as it got away from the heat of the metal. David brought a long strip of gray-looking metal from the supply bag, applied it to the lips of the torn metal, and the boys watched it heat and soften, and then flow as David skillfully applied it down the tear, hammering steadily to smooth out the edge as the rent was filled. In a short while the jet began to take a round, even appearance again, until David finally straightened up, glancing at the sun. "Got another couple of hours—if we can fix that wiring and siding, and pound the landing skid back into place, we might give it a test before dark—"

They worked even faster. Tuck studied the wiring in the engine while David worked on the siding metal. The wires were twisted almost beyond recognition, but Tuck was familiar with wiring of such engines from years of jet scooter building and racing; he went back to the half-track and selected three spools of wire, ripping down the insulation to examine the fine strands of copper and silver. Then he came back, and slowly began rewiring the torn and shredded masses of wires, squatting down, his hands clumsy in the unaccustomed padded fingers of the suit. He soon found there was no way to grab the wires with his fingers satisfactorily. After some experimentation with pliers, wire and welding rod, he worked out a fair approximation of the re-mote-control pincers he had seen used in radioactives lab to manipulate the wires and the contacts. He was thoroughly engrossed in his work, so engrossed that he became oblivious of himself, or the ship, or anything but the delicate and demanding task at hand—

And then, a bolt of fear went through him as he heard a little musical *ping* in his earphones. His hands froze and he sat staring, listening, almost fascinated—

Ping—ping—ping—ping—ping—ping—ping—ping—ping-pingpingpingpingping—

It was a gentle sound, and a terrifying sound, a sound that meant that horrible death was near, hovering over his shoulder—the sound every spaceman had had condi-tioned into his very soul—the sound that said better than any words: *get inside, fast, your circulation is down, your feet are getting cold, too cold—*

Tuck jumped up with a cry, tried to run for the half-track. He could feel the numb coldness around his feet and legs now, and he stumbled and fell heavily. The warmth of the pressure suit was deceptive, it was all too easy to forget that he was working in an atmosphere so cold that his own expired air would freeze into a choking blob in his throat if he were unprotected. He struggled to his feet, shouting to David as he ran, and clambered stiffly into the half-track; then he leaned out to motion David frantically. David stared at him for a moment; then he too came running. Together they fran-tically slammed down the plastic top, sealed it tight. David snapped on the engine controls and the pumps began to work against the deadly cold, letting the en-gine heat in once more around their feet. Tuck sat pant-ing, his heart racing, his feet tingling and burning with a strange kind of pain. And then the boys looked at each other, and burst out laughing, more in relief than any-thing else. "We should have kept an eye on the time," David panted. "Shouldn't have been out there more than two hours at a stretch without warming up. And I forgot you aren't as used to the cold as I am—"

Tuck clutched his side, still gasping for breath. "Scared me to death," he choked. "They've made movies of the helpless spaceman, marooned on an Asteroid with his engines dead, and that nasty little bell was the sound track."

"There are lots of spacemen who can thank that little bell for their lives. It doesn't give them much time, but it does give them *some*."

Tuck shook his head. "You must have a terrible time in the colony, with the cold."

"Not too much. We're used to a chillier atmosphere than you. And the heat of the refinery keeps the dome warm."

"But the mining tunnels—"

"Forty feet of rock is good insulation."

"That's true. Still—"

"There's a lot worse problem than cold, when it comes to living and working in the colony," said David. "Something that four generations of colonists haven't been able to find an answer to, completely."

"What's that?"

"It may seem funny to you. Claustrophobia. Morbid fear of being closed in. The men get it every now and then down in the tunnels, especially when there's been a recent cave-in. Works on their minds, and as soon as they get to thinking about it, it really hits them. Sometimes they get violent, can't even stand being inside the bubble—"

"But can't you send them back to Earth? Rest cure, something like that?"

"Aw—quit joking."

Tuck's eyes widened. "I'm dead serious!"

"Well, we *could* go back to Earth for vacations, all right—but we couldn't buy food, because nobody would sell us food. We couldn't stay anywhere, because no hotel would take us. And then there's always the risk of being mobbed and lynched—most people don't think a trip to Earth is worth it."

A core of anger began burning in Tuck's mind. "But you must have some sort of protection. After all, Earth is civilized. There are laws protecting people's rights—"

David nodded sourly. "If the people know what their rights are. But that involves education. And we don't have much education out here—oh, sure, the kids in the colony go to a school to learn reading and writing, the lucky ones—and there are apprenticeships in technology and mechanics for the older boys, to teach them to run the mining equipment and the refinery. I was taught enough accounting to help dad with the administration of the colony, and one of my pals is working with Doc Taber, just in case Security doesn't send another doctor out here when Doc is gone. But there hasn't been a colonist boy or girl admitted to an Earth University in over seventy-five years."

"Have they tried to get in?"

David gave him a long look. "Take me, for instance. I wanted to study rocketry—rocket engineering, that was for me. Yes, sir. I wrote the Polytechnic Institute for information. Did they even answer my letter? Ha! They did not. So I wrote Earth Security. They told me I would need a fully accredited high-school education before I could even apply. So I wrote the preparatory schools. Know what they said? They all said, fine, come right along—but you'll have to pay tuition, because you were born and live outside the planetary limits of Earth. Know what the tuition was? More money than my dad's been paid in ten years!"

Tuck's eyes blazed. "They've admitted Mars colony boys without tuition!"

David shrugged. "It was only a stall, I know that. If we could have taken it to court, we might have broken the stall, too. But what if we had? My work wouldn't be good enough. My eyes would be the wrong color.

106

They'd find a way to keep me out. Earth Security has seen to that."

Tuck stared through the plexiglass windshield at the little jet plane across the rocks, feeling sick. "Dad doesn't know what a hornet's nest he's working in—he *couldn't* know. He just doesn't realize these things, he doesn't know the true picture."

"He's in a position to do a lot of good for Titan, if he would—"

Tuck nodded. "If he could be made to understand. Look—you told me you had a plan—"

"That's right. I've already set it in motion. I've let the Big Secret out of the bag—to you." David scowled, and started to tighten down his helmet. "I think we should get dad and the Colonel together and tell both of them what we've been talking about."

"It might do some good—"

David looked worried. "But the Colonel could send the word straight back to Earth if he didn't want to co-operate—"

"He wouldn't if we made him promise before we told him."

"Would he keep his vromise?"

Tuck bit his lip. "He's never broken a promise to me before. Never."

David nodded, his eyes bright again. "It might work. It might at least clear the air. All we've got to do is make them sit across the table from each other and talk. And that's all it would take. Just one hour of straight talk—" He glanced down at Tuck's legs. "How are they feeling?"

"Warmed up now."

"Good. Let's give this buggy a trial."

They climbed out in the dimming light, and worked feverishly. After interminable minutes, Tuck got the last wire in place. He looked at it critically, finding no fault, then waved at David. "I think it's ready on this end."

David drove the final rivet, and nodded, eying the narrow gully into which the ship was nosing. It was strewn with boulders and jagged rocks. Tuck jerked a thumb at the half-track. "Why don't we bulldoze a take-off path?"

Together they searched for a large stone with a flat side, and brought the 'track over to it; in a few moments they had it chained securely to the front of the machine, and started the half-track moving down the gully with the rock as a bulldozer blade, shoving rocks and debris to either side with an incredible crashing and flying of rock and snow. The half-track engine whined and roared like a tormented thing, bucking and heaving against the load of rock, but finally they had left behind them a fairly level path, and David studied it, and nodded with satisfaction. "That should do it, if the jet holds, and doesn't warp too much. You stay in the 'track and be ready to duck if I start to spin."

Slowly David clambered into the cockpit of the *Snooper*, pulling the patched hood down over his head. Tuck moved back, suddenly tense. He watched with his heart in his throat as the whining sound of the priming engines suddenly began, muffled, as though far in the distance. For almost five minutes the whine remained steady, then suddenly revved up to the familiar earsplitting squeal of the jet motor. If only nothing went wrong? Deep in his heart, Tuck longed to sit at the controls of that little ship, to head out from the colony, flying low, with telescopic scanner searching out and exploring every crack and crevice. He would have to wait until David offered him the controls, but he could almost feel them in his hands, almost feel the nose of the ship lift, slick as a whistle, sliding up into the dark blue sky—

The jets coughed blue flame, then settled down to a steady pencil-thin streak, so hot Tuck could almost imagine it scorching his eyebrows. With a sudden thrust the little ship jerked, then began sliding down the bull-dozed trough, riding the skids smoothly, faster and faster. And then, like magic, it rose in a burst of speed, the nose lifted, and the ship skimmed off the ground, up and up in a slightly weaving course; in an instant it was clear, skimming into the air like a graceful bird, moving up in a wide arc, curving back down overhead with a squeal of thunder, and off again like lightning in the direction of the colony.

Tuck waited, his heart pounding with excitement. It worked! A little unsteady, a lot that should be done before it was used for an extensive flight, but it was flying! He leaned back in the half-track seat, waiting impatiently for David to return. The minutes ticked by—five, ten. He shifted in the seat, peering anxiously at the rapidly darkening horizon, a flicker of fear in his mind. Fifteen minutes—and then the ship squealed back overhead again, and slid down in a long arc to land on a level stretch beyond the rocks, just as the sun fell beneath the horizon. The pale light of Saturn threw the rocks into weird relief; Tuck snapped on the emergency lamp, swung it along the dark ground until it picked up David hurrying across the jagged rocks on foot. But it wasn't until David was actually climbing up into the 'track that Tuck saw the paleness of his face, the worried wrinkles around his eyes.

David slammed down the hood and sealed it without a word, revving the engine at the same time. Then he said, "Better hold on tight, my friend. We're going to run for it—"

Alarm exploded in Tuck's mind. "What's wrong?"

"Something inside the dome. It looks like the whole colony is assembling in the main hall—"

"Cortell?"

David nodded grimly, and the half-track started with a jerk. "I don't like it. I could see the people coming up to the hall—and they didn't look very peaceful—"

Chapter 11

THE ULTIMATUM

THE TRIP back to the colony was a nightmare that Tuck was to remember as long as he lived. The darkness settled like a cloak, blacking out the sky more and more as the glowing, ringed planet that hung in the sky sank farther and farther toward the horizon, throwing a weird, deceptive gloom over the path. The emergency lamp flickered and blinked, hiding the deep crevices in a limbo of shadow and half-light, turning the rocks into undistinguishable black blobs that suddenly resolved into light and shadow only when the half-track was upon them. They tried to follow their tracks; David huddled grimly over the steering bar, panting and struggling, twisting it as the car lurched and shuddered. Once they struck a huge boulder with an earsplitting crash, and a shower of rocks and boulders hailed down on the plastic top. A little later the caterpillar tracks slipped on a steep, angled grade, and the 'track slid crashing down into a crevice, lodging tight at a ridiculous angle. David threw the engine into four-wheel drive; the soft pillow wheels in front spun as though embedded in thick jelly, until the 'track lurched, and lurched, and finally gave the caterpillars some traction, and the car lumbered out. Not a word was exchanged between the boys. David fought the bar in a frenzy of silent desperation, and Tuck gripped the safety bar for dear life, trying to protect his head from banging on the overhead or the front panel. He felt numb; he tried to think of what David had said, but his thoughts were incoherent. A meeting at the colony could mean a dozen things, a hundred things. What if

Cortell had called a convention? The men were angry, excited—could there be a mob meeting to break Anson Torm's power, for the last crushing blow? Or could it be an attack on the Colonel, turned upon him when he was helpless and alone in the colony? It didn't make sense, nothing made sense as Tuck held on tightly in the lurching vehicle, and he just sat, praying that the half-track would not get stuck somewhere on the way—

It seemed hours before they mounted the final rise and started down the valley toward the colony. The lights were bright; the bubble gleamed like a magic thing in the blackness, but when they reached the lock, a single man was the only human being in sight. The man admitted them, thrusting his thumb over his shoulder. "Better step on it," he shouted as the boys climbed out. "Down in the hall—there's a general colony meeting going on—"

"Who called it?"

"Petition. Two hundred signatures. And it sounds like it's hot as ore slag—"

"Who was pushing the petition?" David struggled out of his pressure suit, panting, his face white.

"Well, it wasn't your father, you can bet on that. Cortell has been out of hiding, down in the mines—him and some of his men. Been going through the mines all day, whipping the men up until they're fighting mad." The guard gave Tuck Benedict a black look from the corner of his eyes, and lowered his voice to a whisper. "He's been telling them that Anson's made a dirty deal with that Earthman—"

David's face whitened, and he started at a run for the hall, Tuck close at his heels. The colony was deserted; every cabin was empty, the lights burning stark in the gloom; the porch of the trading post was empty. Down the road two children were wandering, hand in hand, whimpering, and somewhere far away, Tuck heard a baby squalling, a tiny, helpless, lonely voice shrilling in the darkness. The boys reached the stairs and plunged

111

down, and then at the bottom they stopped and wormed their way into the crowd of excited people. The meeting was in progress.

The room was filled, every seat, every bench. At the head of the room Anson Torm sat at the table, a huge service revolver on the table in front of him; the electric lights were dim, and someone had erected two huge torches that burned smokily on either side of the room, making flickering shadows dance along the rough-hewn walls. Colonel Benedict was also in the front of the room, sitting to one side, his face an angry mask. And standing up in the center of the room was a huge, burly man, talking in a heavy bass rumble. The man held a hat in his hand, and his words were greeted with a mutter of approval from people on all sides.

"—All I know is what I can see, Anson," the big man was saying, wrenching his hat nervously in his hands. "I been with you right down the line—you know that's a fact. But what Cortell says is beginning to sound just about right."

"You mean what Cortell's stooges have been spreading around the colony—is that right?" Anson Torm's voice cut like a knife in the still air.

"I got eyes," the miner snapped back. "What I see is you and this Earthman throwin' Cortell in jail, and holdin' secret meetings. I don't like it. Maybe I don't think Cortell's always right, but he's a colonist, and he's got the good of the colony at heart—"

"*And that's more than some people can say,*" a voice snarled from the rear. A dozen men burst into angry approval. "What have you got to say, Anson?" somebody shouted. "Cortell says you're selling us out—"

Another man jumped to his feet, shaking his fist. "You've been whining around this Earthman's feet for two days now—where has it got you? You've been saying there'd be changes, that Security would listen to us when they sent a man out—well, how about it? Where are the teachers for our kids? And the money for the

112

new school—how about that, Anson?" The man's face was bitter. "What about the building materials they've promised us for years, so we wouldn't have to live in these hovels? When are they going to send us the men we need to run this place so we don't have to work sixteen-hour days?"

Torm's eyes flashed angrily. "Do you think I can help Security's broken word? Who do you think is stopping all these things? *Me?* Do you think *I* am?"

The man on the floor raised his hand and pointed at Colonel Benedict. "That's the man that's doing it—and you're playing right along with him! He's got the power and authority to get changes made if he feels like it. But he doesn't feel like it. All we hear is more work and less food." He turned his eyes to the crowd, waving his hands wildly. "Well I say throw 'em both out! Shut down the mines for a while, and see how Earth Security likes it. I say let's go along with Cortell—"

A cheer went up in the room. Another man was on his feet—it was Taggart, the man Tuck had seen making the rounds of the cottages after Cortell's escape. "Seems to me there are two men to blame," he said, his voice very loud and smooth. Faces turned to him, angry faces. "The one of them is just a spy, an ordinary stooge like all of them Security sends out to crack down harder on the whip. But the other one is worse than any spy could be—" His eyes caught Anson's face, and he stabbed a hand at him, savagely. "That's the man you want to watch. We can fight Earth—and we can win! Don't listen to the old man; listen to the one that's on your side. We can blow up the mines and starve them for power— we could have done it years ago, but oh, no, Torm handed us lots of nice words and pretty promises. Well, the time to break it off with Earth is now. Suicide? Hogwash! Blow up these mines, and Earth is stripped! And even if it *is* suicide—" he paused, glaring around the room. "Well, we've got fathers and grandfathers who died for this colony—what's wrong with you? Are you

113

afraid? Have they got you cowed? Torm is the traitor—let's throw him out, send him back to Earth with his spy friends, and let a *man* lead the colony like it ought to be led—"

Torm stood up slowly, his face very tired. With a trembling hand he banged on the table for silence. Then he said, "In six months the laws governing this colony call for a convention of all colonists asd a general election—either to confirm the old leader, or elect a new one. That's the law—you voted for it; you laid it down. When that election comes, it'll be you who does the voting and you can vote for the Devil himself, for all I care. But until then, I'm still the leader here, with the power to sign warrants and enforce law. And I say John Cortell has attempted murder. I say he'll stand trial for it, and anyone who's helping him will stand trial. *Shut up, Taggart,* you've had your say, just the way Cortell told you to say it. Now I'll have mine."

He brushed a hand over his forehead, and leaned forward, both hands on the table. "You've done a great job tonight," he said bitterly. "A great job. You expect Earth Security to trust us, to give us more freedom, more education, more respect—and then you put on a show like this. Well, it won't work. You want to go along with Cortell's insanity—well, that won't work, either. It's suicide. What you're talking about is the end of the line. And as long as I'm leader, I won't let you do that—"

Taggart was on his feet again. "We've had about enough of your soft talk, Anson. How about, it men? Are we going to wait for an election? Cortell says the time is *now*—are we going to give this Earth spy six months to get a nice fleet of Security Patrol ships out here to fight us?"

One of Torm's men jumped to his feet, hands in pockets, avoiding Anson's eyes. "Now wait a minute, Taggart—we've got to go slow. This—this all is happening too fast." He looked unhappily at the colony leader.

"Anson, I've been with you, too—but now I don't know. We're in too deep now. Cortell's plan is risky, I admit that—but you can see for yourself—" he gestured helplessly.

"Attaboy!" Taggart shouted. "How about some more of Torm's men? Carter, Aaronstein? Miller? What have you got to say?"

"I say you're a pack of fools!" Ned Miller shouted, jumping up on a chair so he could be seen. "This colony has never had a better leader, and you know it. Cortell's plan *risky?* Is cutting your throat risky? You're fools, the whole crowd of you—"

The whole room was explosive now; Tuck caught David's arm, whispered sharply in his ear. "We've got to do something! This place is going wild!"

David shook his head desperately. "We can't. There's no time—"

Tuck saw his father, sitting like a statue, his face bleak. He looked tired and old, as though the life had been torn from him, and he was a corpse sitting there in the front of the room. Then suddenly Colonel Benedict came to life; he slammed his fist down on the table, and stood up, bitter anger heavy on his face. He was dressed in full Security uniform, and he stood proudly, his back straight, gray hair perfectly combed, mustache crisp above thin-drawn lips. This was the picture that was so familiar, Tuck thought, the picture of Earth that the colonists had, and hated so much. The Colonel stepped in front of the table, and the uproar subsided, reluctantly, every eye turning to the Colonel's face.

"I've heard about as much of this as I want to hear," he said quietly, and his voice held a whiplash in its softness. "I don't care a hang whether you consider me a spy from Earth, which I am not, or a legal, authorized delegate of the Earth Security Commission, which I am. I do not care a nickel whom you elect as your leader, or what kind of petty little squabbles you insist upon having in this colony. But as far as what you do in the

115

mines is concerned, I've heard enough nonsense in this room tonight to last me for the rest of my life."

The Colonel paused, his eyes sweeping the room. "These mines are going to continue to run, no matter what happens here. If you threaten production from these mines, Security is prepared to throw every man, woman and child in the colony into prison for treason, and send you back to Earth for trial, and bring in convicts and soldiers to run the mines. Already there's been violence—my own life has been threatened twice. There'd better not be any more."

The crowd exploded into an angry roar. Anson Torm was on his feet, turning furiously to the Colonel. "Can't you see that threats won't frighten these people any more? They've been living under threats for years. They won't take any more."

"They are threatening Earth's entire economy. And they seem to have an exalted opinion of their own importance, for some strange reason." The Colonel's voice was like a knife.

"But if they blow up the mines—"

"And kill themselves at the same time? I'm sorry, but that bluff won't work. Too many people have been trying to bluff me—"

Pandemonium broke loose on the floor as a dozen men began shouting at once. "You must be blind," Torm cried. "Do you really think these people are bluffing?"

"Five hundred people will not deliberately blow up the very colony they must have in order to survive. Yes, I think they're bluffing." He straightened up, and his voice cut through the rising growl of the colonists. "I want Cortell in irons, and I want him on the Earth ship." He was shaking with anger, his voice trembling. "I don't care who wins your little battle here. But I want Cortell delivered to me at the Rocket Landing by sundown tomorrow. If he isn't there then, and if you aren't back in the mines then, I'll declare martial law in this colony, and call a troopship in from Ganymede to enforce it."

116

The Colonel turned to Torm as a horrified hush fell over the room. "Do I make myself perfectly clear?"

"Perfectly." Torm spat the word, as though it were something disgraceful.

"Then if you don't mind, I'll leave you to your squabbling." The Colonel turned away contemptuously. "I'd like a half-track placed at my disposal immediately."

He strode through the crowd like a man apart, catching Tuck's eye as he passed, nodded grimly toward the stairs. Tuck followed him silently, his heart sinking. "Where are we going?"

"Back to the ship. It isn't safe to remain here now."

"But Dad, this is all wrong—"

"And I'll thank you to keep your nose out of it, if you please!" His father's voice was furious. Without another word he strode up the stairs.

Tuck hesitated just a moment, trying to catch David's eye. But when he saw the utter despair on the boy's face, he turned quickly and followed his father.

Minutes later they were walking swiftly toward the colony air lock.

Chapter 12

A DESPERATE CHANCE

FOR A LONG time they rode in silence. The half-track had been waiting for them when they gathered their belongings from the Torms' cabin, Tuck packing in despair, his father in white-faced anger. They had climbed in, with the Colonel at the steering bar, and the vehicle started out across the valley floor in the direction of the Rocket Landing.

Tuck had no idea what time it was, but he knew it was very late. Saturn had set now; the sky was pitch black, matching perfectly the black rocks of the tundra. There seemed to be no hurry; the Colonel eased the half-track along, searching out the path with the emergency lamp, frequently slowing to a stop to study the treacherous ground. Tuck sat huddled on the seat, his mind whirling with the sudden turn of events. For the first time in his life he felt himself utterly at a loss—there seemed to be no possible answer. He stared miserably out the front panel, saying over and over to himself that this was all wrong, that there *had* to be an answer—but he realized that his father still didn't know about the Big Secret—whatever it was. And as he watched the Colonel, sitting stiffly, face still angry, Tuck knew he couldn't tell him now. Several times he started to speak; each time it suddenly seemed ridiculous. There was nothing to say, as minute by minute they moved farther away from the colony.

Finally Tuck said, "There must be *some* way to stop them."

"A trial for treason will stop them," the Colonel snapped. "Of all the pigheaded, rebellious trash I ever saw in my life—"

"You haven't given them a chance—"

The Colonel snorted, turning angry eyes to his son. "Yes, they seem to have you right along with them. I thought you had more sense than to swallow their nonsense."

Tuck's eyes widened. "What did I do?"

"You really gave me a helping hand, you did, getting yourself all chummy with that ninny of a son of his. That was fine. While I was doing everything I could to keep things on a negotiable basis, you had to pour fuel on Cortell's little fire, to make the people think that a shady deal was going on. I wonder what kind of friends you picked back at school."

Tuck's ears turned red at the sarcasm. "I'm sorry, Dad. But you aren't even trying to see their viewpoint at all—"

"They have no viewpoint that makes any difference!" The Colonel burst out angrily. "You'd think they'd feel some sort of loyalty to the land that feeds them, and supports them and depends on them. Viewpoint, bah! First they try to blackmail me, and then they take my own son out and feed him a wild story that he doesn't have brain enough to see through—"

"That isn't fair, and you know it!"

The Colonel looked at Tuck, and his face softened suddenly. The anger disappeared, and left behind it lines of weariness and defeat. "Oh, I suppose it isn't. You didn't know any better, and probably David didn't realize what he was doing, either. I—I'm just tired, that's all. He sighed audibly. "This thing beats me, Tuck. It doesn't make sense. I came up here to try to make a peaceable settlement, and I haven't gotten to first base. Everything's gone wrong right from the first, and now it looks like it's going to be the end. We'll be back to the penal colony stage, after all these years, and that's a real defeat." He shook his head wearily. "I don't know. Maybe I'm getting old."

Tuck sat in silence, his heart sinking. Then his father really *didn't* realize what the true picture was. He still thought the whole business was a huge scheme to bluff him—with Torm and Cortell and David all working together. A flicker of doubt passed through his mind. Could it be possible that he *had* been fooled? That David *had* been used to foment violence against Torm and his father? Could it be that the Big Secret was actually ready, and that Torm himself was trying to breed an "incident" that would make it necessary to use it? Tuck shook his head. He just couldn't believe that. Because there was no retreat for the colonists, no matter what plan they had. They could only go underground, into some vast subterranean vault, to lock themselves in, if they rebelled against Earth. Earth was too powerful, it spread too far. And once the die was cast, no Titan colonist would ever again be able to go anywhere in the Solar System. Their names would be the names of traitors against humanity, and they would have to stay in their hole and rot. So perhaps they would survive for twenty years, or fifty years, or a hundred years—what good was survival that way?

No, David was right, and the Colonel was wrong. He could see that—his father couldn't. The Colonel had brought a little more distrust, a little deeper prejudice, and a more bitter fund of experience with him. These were the things that blocked his father and blinded him. He couldn't see what had been happening to the Titan colonists, he couldn't realize what it meant to live in a tight, crowded, frozen colony for generation after generation, seeing their slender grip on freedom and their rights as men being torn from them bit by bit.

120

He couldn't understand how they could be as desperate as they really were. And if Tuck were to tell him about the Big Secret—the Colonel would probably laugh. Because unless he could see the colonists' viewpoint, the Big Secret would be just another deceit, just another lie to use to blackmail him—

The half-track jounced through the gorge where the ambush had been laid. Tuck and his father peered out, but could see very little of the rubble that had fallen. Minutes passed—how long had they been gone? An hour? Two? Tuck knew he should be tired, but sleep was far from his mind. Slowly they rolled along, moving in a strange slow motion, a little black bug feeling its way across the wastes of an impossible planetoid to the last haven of humanity that still remained—the ship from Earth. Yet once they reached it, there would be no retreat. The colony would be lost. Because Torm would never be able to hold the colonists to his side after this last failure to settle peaceable with Earth.

And the Big Secret: There was the question mark, the key to the whole problem. It kept thrusting itself upon Tuck's mind, insistently, and he reviewed what David had said about it. It seemed incredible that a plan could have been prepared in absolute secrecy for over a hundred years—and what could possibly take so long? What kind of plan could possibly offer the colony any sort of hope whatsoever?

Slowly, as they bounced along, things began to line themselves up in Tuck's mind, like the outlines he had made in school. When you have a problem, write down everything you know about it—all the facts in one column, all the unknowns in another column, all possible solutions in another. Then eliminate.

All right. Problem:

The Big Secret—

A plan, a last-ditch plan, an escape, a way out that

the colonists could use if they were driven against the wall. Check.

A plan that was guided by a very few people, kept in strict secrecy from the rest. Check again.

A plan that had taken over a hundred years to set in readiness. Check.

A plan that would take care of all five hundred people in the colony, a plan that would allow them to *blow up the mines and the colony they had been living in.* Check.

Hold it. Slow now. Something was missing there— Tuck shifted his weight as the half-track slid down a grade, then hit the bottom and lurched up again with a roar. A plan, a last-ditch plan, *a way out*—

A way out that Anson Torm thought was suicide, and risked being branded a traitor to oppose. But Cortell was eager to set it in motion—

A difference of opinion, then. Odd? Very odd. A last-ditch plan that was hazardous, terribly hazardous, but which *might work.* That made sense! There was great risk involved. It might be a way out, or it might be death. Cortell was willing to gamble; Torm was not—

But that meant that it might be a *permanent way out for the colonists, if it worked.* A way out in utter defiance of Earth—

Tuck chewed his lip. An underground station? Could that possibly, even conceivably, be a *permanent* way out?

Never. It just didn't add up.

But what else? A ship to escape in? To escape where? What kind of a ship would carry five hundred people and let them hide out in a Solar System teeming with Security Patrol ships, a ship that would be hunted down to the bitter end. Possible? Even conceivable?

Never. There could be no escape *off the planetoid itself.* There was no place to go, no place to hide.

But *what?* Open war against Earth? Even more ridiculous. There were big enough ruthenium stores on Earth to last for several weeks. The colonists would be wiped out, utterly massacred.

Then what was the Big Secret?

It was something big, and something desperate beyond belief.

It was something *on Titan*.

Therefore—it was something that *could be found*.

Tuck stared at his father, an impossible plan forming in his mind. His father wouldn't listen to reason now, he wouldn't believe anything the colonists told him. Nothing would change his father's attitude at this point but *facts*—cold, clear, unarguable facts. And there was only one fact that would make much difference. The plan. The true nature of the Big Secret. If Tuck could get back to the colony, somehow, contact David there, there might still be time. Time to find the Big Secret, wherever it was, *what*ever it was, and bring back the facts to lay before the two men.

Tuck's heart pounded, and he tensed against the gripping bar, the plan crystallizing in his mind. Carefully he watched his father drive the half-track. He'd never driven it before, but he seemed to be doing all right, and Tuck had watched David drive it. His eyes narrowed thoughtfully. There wasn't any other vehicle at the ship that could travel over this kind of ground. If it were possible—

After a long, unbearable time, the 'track mounted the last rise, and tumbled over the rim, down into the shallow crater where the Earth ship stood, tall and shiny. Already there was a brightening on the horizon—the night was short, and it was almost dawn. Weird shadows were creeping out of the blacks and grays, showing the surface of the valley in more detail.

"We'll need some sleep," the Colonel was saying, "and I think we'd better get it while the getting is good. We'll have the men alerted as soon as anything pops, and have them radio for a troopship from Ganymede right now—it can't be too soon." He glanced over at Tuck. "And I think you'd better stay on the ship, no matter what happens. I've had no right to drag you into this in the first place, particularly since I've made such a nice mess of things. And don't worry too much about your young friend—I've a notion he'll make out all right."

Tuck nodded, his conscience jabbing him sharply. It was a desperate decision, a desperate chance to take, yet he knew he had to take it. It would mean disobeying his father—but there would be no answer but violence and death if he didn't do it. And they could find the answer, if only there were time—

The half-track stopped thirty yards from the crane, and the top sprang open with a hiss. The Colonel clambered out, stepping down to the frigid ground. Tuck leaned back over the seat, as though hunting for something in the storage space, his heart beating in his throat, moving as slowly as he dared, until he saw his father start walking away from the half-track. Then, like lightning, Tuck snapped the switch that slammed the hood back down; in the same motion he started the pump at top speed, its motor roaring in his ears. For the briefest instant he caught a glimpse of his father's face, startled, realization dawning; then he revved up the motor, jerked back on the steering bar, threw the gear into reverse, and felt the vehicle lurch back thirty feet from his father. The Colonel started running toward the vehicle, shouting, and Tuck desperately snapped on the emergency lamp, catching the Colonel full in the face, blinding him for an instant. Then, with a roar, the half-track pivoted, started rolling crazily away from the ship again, headed up the path that led to the colony. Through the back of the hood he saw his father's tiny figure, running after the half-track for a few steps, then stopping, standing still, just staring. And then Tuck wrenched his mind away, forcibly thrust his betrayal out of his mind, concentrated on guiding the lumbering vehicle.

It slipped and slid, jouncing him out of the seat time after time, banging his head on the top, throwing him almost over on his face. It was speed now that counted, speed more than anything else, and he urged the car forward recklessly. A dismal red line was forming on the horizon; dawn was not far away, but the light only confused the picture before him as the half-track hurtled up the grade and over the rim, leaving the Earth ship far behind. Tuck hung on for dear life, praying that the machine would stay upright, and not run into any of the treacherous gullies and crevices that lay on either side.

The *Snooper* was in working order. If he could get to the colony and get David, they could go for the little ship. He had no more idea than the man in the moon what they would be looking for—but *something* existed, the Big Secret was *somewhere*—and if it existed, it could be found—

A squeal of jet engines cut through to his ears, and he braked down the half-track, staring. Like a streak, he saw the little jet swoop down over him, arc up high, and loop over to come in again. Tuck's heart skipped a beat. David had had the same idea! He slowed the 'track to a stop, threw open the hood, and crawled out, running down the grade to the place where the *Snooper* had jetted in.

David waved, and moved aside in the cockpit, motioning Tuck in beside him. "I thought I was going to have to storm the ship single-handed to get you out," he exclaimed. "Your dad really fixed things! I had to sneak out—sent the air-lock guard on a wild-goose chase and copped his half-track to get out to the *Snooper*—"

"But why?"

"I've been thinking, Dad got control of things in the meeting finally—but only because of the fight with the Colonel." He grinned. "Cortell's boys were having trouble explaining why they would be fighting if they were really in cahoots. But there's only one thing that will bring any sort of solution now." He looked up at Tuck, his face eager. "It means selling out my dad and the colony, but it's the only thing."

"You mean the plan," Tuck said eagerly.

"Exactly. Wherever it is, we've got to find it, and spring it wide-open to everybody. If that won't get dad and the Colonel together, nothing will."

Tuck nodded. "It will. It can't help but do it. But where do we start?"

David chewed his lip for a moment. "Wherever it is, it's connected with the colony," he said. "I mean by tunnel. I don't have any idea where. The easiest thing would be to go in through the colony, but I'm afraid that's out. Cortell would have the tunnel guarded, whichever one it was—"

Tuck blinked. "That would tip us off to the right one—"

"If we ever did find it. But there may be another way in."

"From the outside?"

"Right. If it's a vault, or a battle station, it's big—it would have to be to take five hundred people. There are lots of abandoned shafts that might let us into the mines. And once inside, we'll have to make use of every break we can." He snapped on the primer switch of the jet. "Hang on, boy," he said softly. "We've got a lot of hunting to do, and we haven't got much time."

Tuck sat back, hardly able to breathe, the excited whine of the engines driving all thoughts out of his mind. The little scooter jerked, bumped a time or two, and then suddenly they were swooping out into the clear, thin atmosphere, rising higher and higher, until passing even now, precious minutes that could mean they could see the edge of the morning sun. Time was success of failure. With time closing in on them, it seemed an almost impossible chance—

But somewhere below them the planet held a secret, a secret that had been kept inviolate for a hundred years. And in a few short hours, somehow, the secret had to be found—

Chapter 13

THE SECRET OF THE TUNNEL

THE QUEST seemed hopeless from the start. Tuck had never been higher above the surface of Titan than the observation room of the Earth ship; he had never realized the vastness of the place. But now, as the *Snooper* skimmed higher and higher into the sun the realization drove home, and he stared bleakly down at the wild panorama spread out beneath them.

There was no break in the barren wildness. A few miles to the right he could see the oval dome of the colony, reflecting the early morning light, gleaming like a dull jewel as the lights within it blinked off one by one. But the colony lay totally isolated by miles and miles of endless rock. Even as they rose, the surface lost its detail and took on a different sort of wildness. It was a mammoth chunk of barren rock—

And somewhere down there five hundred people had carved out a tiny foothold, and from it were threatening the entire Solar System!

David Torm glanced down for an instant. "Not very pretty, eh?"

"It looks horrible. I don't see how we could ever find anything."

David chuckled. "Don't give up yet." He tipped the nose of the little ship down again, and curved in toward the colony. "We can't see anything at all up this high— I just wanted to give you a picture of the surface." He pointed off toward the rising sun. "The first thing I want to do is to go down there close to the surface and look for a fault I saw a couple of months ago. There was a big clordelkus there—the nasty things like oxygen, for dessert, I guess and he'd sucked up enough stone to start a cave-in over the tunnel. I mapped it, and didn't pay too much attention to it, but it might get us inside the tunnels. If we spot that, so we know we *can* get in, we'll start circling the colony in widening circles. That way we should spot anything that looks suspicious."

"And if we don't see anything?"

"Then we'll try hunting from the inside." The ship was quite low now, sweeping over the jagged land in a beeline for the sun. David handed Tuck a pair of binoculars. "I'll make several runs of about five miles over the area—see if you can spot anything."

"What am I looking for, exactly?"

"A deep cut."

Tuck snorted. "The whole surface is full of deep cuts."

"Sure, I know—but this will be sandbagged up, and you should be able to see the bags." The ship cut even lower, and Tuck started scanning the ground as it whizzed by, looking for anything which might be an artificial cut. The ship reached the end of the run, made a quarter-mile arc, and sped back. The high rocky cliffs spun by them crazily; sometimes the ship jerked up abruptly, sometimes it nearly skidded on the ground, sending up whirlwinds of snow in its wake. Still Tuck saw nothing. He kept gripping at the instrument panel as the ship lurched and dropped, but there was just nothing to see.

"You do a good job of flying," he said, as they skimmed along one of the runs.

"Lots of practice. I'd hoped to get into rocketry, and I learned everything I could from dad's books—but it took a lot of flying hours, too." The leader's son looked over at Tuck. "I'm still going to get into rocketry," he said. "Somehow, I'll get a rocket built. We're in a perfect place to base some real exploratory work here—

study Saturn and her moons, all of them." His eyes took a wistful light. "But that's just the start. Someday, maybe even while I'm alive, somebody is going to break the space barrier. The *real* space barrier—"

Tuck's eyes glowed. "You mean discover an interstellar drive?"

David nodded. "Good old Sol is just one star. There are millions of them waiting for us. When they build the first star-ship—that's where I want to be." He spun the scooter around for another run, then snorted in disgust. "This is getting us nowhere. Let's take the colony as a hub and start circling."

The sun rose higher and higher, a dim, small, feeble-looking sun, glowering out of a cloudless purple sky. Tuck's eyes were smarting from the staring, but he kept the binoculars tight to his pressure helmet. An hour passed as they moved slowly out from the colony in ever-widening circles. Finally he dropped the binoculars disgustedly. "I wouldn't see anything if it walked up and kicked me," he growled. "All I see is gorges and cuts and cliffs—"

"Want to let me look for a while?"

"And let me fly?" Tuck's heart leaped.

"Think you can do it?"

"Of course. I won't go as low as you are, but I can almost match it." He held on as David slid into a long, even stretch, then rose higher and shifted the controls to automatic. The cockpit was a tight squeeze, but they managed to shift, and in a few moments Tuck's hands were gripping the semicircular wheel, and he felt the little scooter responding to every touch, every movement. He brought the ship up in a high arc, exhileration shooting through him to the depths of his bones. His mind went back for a second to the obstacle races he had flown back in school; then he brought the ship in low. He found the place where they had left their circles, and closed in, picking up a landmark in each quarter turn every time around, moving slowly outward. The colony grew farther and farther away as the minutes lengthened into another hour, and his hopes dwindled with every minute—

"Wait—" David stared into the binoculars, shifting around as the ship left the ground behind. "Wait a minute—"

"See something?"

David scowled. "Can't tell. Bring her in very low, right over that stretch there—see the gorge running off at two o'clock? Try to follow it." His voice was excited, and he peered down, holding the binoculars ready. Tuck swung the ship around and brought her in, scooping down as low as he dared. He could pay no attention to anything but the path the ship was taking, and he saw the walls of the gorge rise up on either side as they skimmed through. And then David let out a yip of glee. "Here," he cried. "Let me take it. See what you see! Just this side of the gorge, over to the right—"

Tuck relinquished the controls, peered through the binoculars at the jagged ground below. At first he could see nothing; then, as they swooped over, he saw what looked like a deep, black, perfectly rectangular hole—

"Looks like a cave-in!" he cried.

"Looks like it."

"Is this the one you saw?"

"Nope. This is lots farther out."

"Think we can get into it?"

"We can sure try!" He slid the ship down, searching for a smooth place to land. "At any rate, we'll take a look. This may be our way into the tunnels." He was busy at the controls for a few moments, and then the ship was down, and the sound of the jets was dying away in their ears. In a moment they were out, lumbering for the fault as fast as their clumsy suits would let them—

The hole was about thirty feet deep, perfectly rectangular at the top, but sloping up from the bottom on one side, as though one section of the tunnel had given way, and a landslide piled into it. As they stared, they could see at the bottom an opening, leading into a black hole that seemed to disappear into the wall of rock.

"It *is* a tunnel!" David was scrambling down the side, staring at the other side of the hole. Tuck hesitated.

"Seems odd there isn't an alarm, if it goes into the tunnels—"

David shook his head. "Not so strange. The colony end of the tunnel is completely blocked off by the cave-in. This must open into the outer end."

Tuck peered down at him. "You think it's cut off from the main tunnel back to the colony?"

David nodded. "And look there—" He pointed to a large chunk of smoothly scooped-out rock lying in the debris. "Looks like we can thank our little silicon friend for this, too. Probably this cave-in is quite recent—"

"Shall we go in?"

"Might as well—even if it is a dead end." David climbed down to the bottom of the slide, cleared rocks away from the black hole, and stuck his head in. A moment later he looked back. "Come on. This goes quite a way in."

Tuck clambered down, careful not to cut his pressure suit on the jagged rocks. Together they struggled through the tunnel, snapping on their helmet lamps as the darkness closed in on them. The tunnel was seven or eight feet high, and four feet wide, beamed heavily on the sides and overhead. Thirty yards ahead it curved to the left and disappeared into the darkness.

David stopped after a few steps, and turned to Tuck, a strange expression in his eyes. "Wait a minute," he said softly.

"What's wrong?" Tuck's voice was a startled whisper.

"Everything!" David whispered back. "I've been thinking. I don't remember any tunnel here. No tunnel of any sort. I've studied all the maps, and the maps say that there's a large vein of radioactives between here and the colony—and no way to dig through it safely—"

132

Tuck's eyes widened. "This is a tunnel, map or no map—" He stopped short, staring over his shoulder at the little path of light, then back at David. "You mean—"

"Has your Geiger been acting up since we came in here?"

"Not a peep."

"That's what I thought. There's a tunnel through here, all right, but not through any radioactive vein, and not on any map that *I've* ever seen!" He jerked his head and started down the tunnel. "Buddy, we're on to something!"

They plodded on in silence. The stillness of the place was oppressive, almost ghostly; their footsteps echoed and re-echoed in the darkness. As the tunnel curved, the opening to the outside disappeared, and they were in total darkness except for the flicker of their helmet lamps.

"Look!" said David suddenly.

Forty feet ahead the tunnel suddenly broke into a Y. One branch curved gently off to the left, and then down. The other cut sharply to the right. And at the junction was a large, dull metal object.

Tuck stopped short and stared. "What is it?"

"A pump and blower. There have been cave-ins before in this tunnel—and that means it's an old one. And look at the beaming—wooden! They haven't beamed tunnels with wood for years."

"Let's split up here," said Tuck. "I'll take the right, you take the left. Will the phones carry through this rock?"

"For a little way."

"All right. Look—let's each walk for ten minutes. Then come back. Meet me here in twenty minutes."

"That's good," said David. "There's something about this I don't like."

Tuck waved and started down the right-hand tunnel. It cut very sharply around, then suddenly straightened. Tuck walked slowly, the only sound those of his own footsteps. He shivered, suddenly, as he walked. A tunnel where there was no tunnel on the map—beyond a radio-active bed that didn't exist. His heart pounded wildly. It could be only one thing. But what if they were caught down here, snooping into some strange underground vault that had been kept deadly secret for a century—what could they do? Tuck realized with a jolt that he hadn't thought of weapons. With the tunnel open to the outside, a quick blow to smash his helmet would be the end—

The tunnel widened suddenly, and he was in a small room, packed to the ceiling with sandbags. And against one wall were boxes—he peered at them, curiously. They were aluminum cargo boxes, stacked one on top of another. Every box had a stencil on its side that read, "Titan Colony, via Rocket Freight," followed by a date—

"Tuck!"

Tuck started violently as the cry burst into his ear-phones, and his heart pounded in his throat.

"What's the matter, Dave?"

And then there was an excited shout in the 'phones that Tuck couldn't catch, and he heard the jog-jog-jog coming through of running feet in the other tunnel. He turned and rushed back down the tunnel toward the Y again, a thousand horrible phantoms welling up in his mind. His suit was clumsy; his feet slipped once, and he went crashing to the ground, a sharp pain wrenching at his shoulder, but he dragged himself up again, and rushed on. At the Y he ran into David head-on, frantic with excitement. "I've found it," David choked between gasps. "Come on, *I've found it*—"

He started back up the left-hand tunnel, with Tuck hard on his heels. The tunnel curved, and then dipped down, running straight for a hundred feet or more. Then David slowed down, waving him to a halt. Up ahead was an opening into *something* with gloomy gray light filtering out. But David was pointing to the strip of dull gray material that ran across the tunnel, three strips

134

that blended almost perfectly with the uneven ground, arranged just close enough together so that anyone not watching the path carefully would step on one of the strips, with the little shiny metal detonator caps that followed the strips—

"Murexide!"

David nodded. "I barely spotted it." Gingerly he stepped between the strips, then across to the other side, and Tuck followed, his heart in his throat. A perfect booby trap for one who wasn't watching closely for just such a thing. On the other side they hesitated for a moment; then David urged him on with a wave of a hand, and they hurried again toward the opening, and stopped short, almost teetering on the drop that lay before them. And they stood there and stared, peering dumbfounded at the incredible thing they saw there before them in the gloom—

It was not a vault, nor a battle station, nor even a stockade. *It was a ship*, standing upright on its jets in a tall, narrow crevice, with the open top camouflaged and sealed with gray plastic sheeting that blended perfectly into the rock. A pale gray light filtered down from above, and the huge ship stood like a ghost, tall and silent in the gloom—

Tuck stared at David, dumbfounded. "But—but a *ship!* But there's no place to *go* with a ship! They'd be hunted down, if it took a thousand years. *There's no place in the Solar System they could hide*—" His voice broke off with a gasp as the implication of his own words struck him.

There was only one place where a ship would be beyond pursuit. Completely and utterly beyond pursuit.

There was only one conclusion possible.

The ship was a star ship.

Chapter 14

TRAPPED!

Tuck Benedict and David Torm stared at the ship in the gloomy crevice, stared speechless at the long, slender form as the implication sank in. And then they were both talking at once, forgetting where they were in their amazement at the ship in the crevice before them. A thousand questions roared through Tuck's brain, a thousand pressing questions, questions that came out with incredible, staggering answers.

"But where could they have *gotten* it? There's never been a ship like this on Titan for anything except regular cargo runs—and how *could* it be a star-ship? How could it take five hundred people—"

"I don't know, but this is the plan—it must be." David stared up at the long, slender, finger-like structure. "It must be the Earth ship that crashed. That was a troopship—built to carry three or four hundred men—"

"But that was lost clear around on the other side of the planet!"

"I know. But the Security Patrol never found it, did they?"

"No—it was an impossible task. Titan is almost half as big as Earth. What chance would a search party have? The ship may have fallen into one of those gorges, and covered over with frost so it was completely invisible from above."

David Torm nodded. "But everyone knew a ship had crashed. There was no colony here then—but when the

136

colonists first worked out the plan, they *knew* there was a ship—somewhere—"

"And they must have found it." Tuck's voice was filled with awe. "They must have torn it apart, bit by bit, hull plate by hull plate, tube by tube—and brought it here."

David jumped up, excitedly. "That's right! Just a few men, working in secret, dragging all that metal clear around from the other side. And then they found this crevice here to reassemble it—and it's taken them a hundred years."

Tuck shook his head, still incredulous. "And the tunnel?"

"They must have built it in secret, and then made up a story about a vein of radioactives to keep the other colonists—and the Earthmen—away." He stared down the black hole where the jet tubes disappeared, and the fins on which the ship rested.

"It still doesn't add up!" Tuck burst out. "Where did they get an interstellar drive for it? The greatest minds in the world have been working on Earth for two hundred years to find a drive that would take a ship to the stars. They've had laboratories, money, government support—and *they've never found it*. They say it's theoretically impossible." He turned to David, his eyes wide. "How could the *colonists* have found something that all Earth's technology couldn't find?"

David shrugged. "I couldn't even guess."

"Well, I'll tell you one thing—*I want to see those engines!*"

"I don't know if we should go on board her or not—" All of a sudden David was trembling. "I don't like this, Tuck—I'm scared of what'll happen if they find us—"

"If the colonists have developed an interstellar drive, *it's in that ship*. You can stay here if you want. I'm going in." Tuck started up the ramp toward the dark port in the ship's side. David hesitated, then started up after him. "Look," he said, pointing upward at the scaffolding. "They're still finishing the hull plates. They must have built it from the inside out. And it looks almost finished—"

They stepped from the ramp into the ship, and Tuck felt a thrill unlike anything he had ever experienced. Here was the adventure he had dreamed of all his life; here was the ship that was built to go to the stars, built to leave Earth and Earth's puny Solar System light-years behind, built to speed straight as an arrow—where? Alpha Centaurus? Cygni? Acturus? Here was the greatest frontier of all, the frontier that had never been crossed —the frontier physicists on Earth had said *could never be crossed*—

Because there was no drive for an interstellar ship. The weeks and months in transit between Earth and Mars or Venus or Titan on fast Interplanetary Atomics were insignificant compared to the years—the centuries —that would be required to travel with them to the stars. Man's life was too short to make such a trip possible without an interstellar drive.

And yet, in the bowels of this strange secret ship— was the drive there? Could the colonists, in their desperation, have discovered genius in their midst, genius to solve the immense mathematical and technical impossibilities of a space-warp, of faster-than-light motion? The boys made their way along the narrow dark corridor of the ship, moving downward, still downward to the rear of the ship. They passed a huge room, and stopped, peering through the hatch at the tier upon tier of soft, curved mattresses, set at 45° angles from the floor— the acceleration cots. This was the troop hold, the quarters that had been built to carry the Security Patrol troops, over a century ago—how many were there? The boys stopped, and counted the cots on the first row, and counted the number of tiers. Five hundred. The ship was to carry the entire colony. There was no doubt of it.

Then in another room a bright light shone, and when they walked in, they found a sealed lock and an inner hatch. They moved curiously into the lock, and sealed the door behind them, heard the automatic pumps whir, until the inner hatchway sprang open, and they walked into a brilliant flare of lights. It was a large room, lined with mercury vapor lamps and carbon arcs, a room so damp and hot that their cold suits were drenched with water, and they stood in little individual rainstorms, until they could peer through their dripping helmets at the row upon row of green things, growing plants in huge tanks. The hydroponic tanks—to provide growing food, to cleanse the great ship of carbon dioxide and to replenish the feeble stores of oxygen the ship could carry for five hundred people. They wiped the water from their suits in sheets, and moved back through the lock. Out once again in the icy corridor the water froze in solid sheets upon them, and tinkled and crashed to the floor as they broke it off. But still they moved to the rear, on toward the wonderful engines that lay in the bowels of the ship.

Tuck knew the layout of the ship; he had explored the Earth ship in minute detail during the passage out to Titan, and was familiar with what to expect of such ships. But David had never before traveled on a rocket ship; his acquaintance had been confined to a brief visit now and then, and he followed Tuck with open mouth and wide eyes, finding amazement in every turn of the passageway, excitement in every compartment. And when they opened the hatch that led to the engine rooms and generators David could hardly believe that a single ship could carry propelling engines so huge.

But Tuck didn't wait for his friend. In an instant he was down among the generators, examining the engines, moving swiftly from one great pile of machinery to another, eyes growing wider, more incredulous by the minute. And when David finally caught up with him, he found the Earth boy sitting stunned on an auxiliary generator, staring about in bewilderment. "What's wrong, boy? Are you sick?"

"Sick? No—no. I'm—I'm fine. I—I just can't understand it—"

David glanced around nervously. "Understand what?"

Tuck stared up at him, hollow-eyed. "*The engines!*"

"What's wrong with the engines?"

"There's nothing wrong with them. They're perfectly good, common, ordinary, everyday interplanetary atomics. *There isn't any interstellar drive on this ship!*"

David sat down heavily. "I thought not. Because if there were, it would be easy for them to escape. And my father thought it would be suicide for them—"

Tuck nodded, speaking almost as if he were in an unbelievable dream. "It would be suicide. They would have to make this ship a colony—a permanent colony, drifting endlessly in space. They would have to take their bearings, and head out into deep space until their power gave out—and then they would have to drift. They would keep going, and they would reach their star—someday. But it would take three hundred years." He looked up at David. "Do you realize what that would mean? That would be *twelve generations* to live and die aboard this ship before it reached its destination! And what might they find, even if they reached it? A planet they could live on? Who knows? There might not be any planets in the system they reached—or there might not be any oxygen, any food. They would never know until they got there—and they might never even survive to reach it—it would be almost hopeless to try and support five hundred people, and their children, and their children's children, on a ship like this for three hundred years."

David nodded. "But there would be a chance."

"A chance? What kind of a chance? A billion to one?"

"More chance than staying here. Because at least the colony would be free."

Tuck stared at the engines about them. "Do you think that they would actually try it?"

David nodded, very slowly. "I know my people," he

said. "Even a billion-to-one chance at freedom would be better, to them. But only if there was no hope here."

"But Cortell is urging them into it now!"

"Cortell is a fool. He wants to lead, and he hates Earth—more than anything else in his life, he hates Earth. He wants to stop the mines, destroy Earth's power, no matter what the cost. And this is the way he can do it."

They sat in silence for a few minutes. Then Tuck said, "There's still time to stop him. The ship isn't loaded completely; there is still the whole colony and their clothes and supplies to load. We've still got a little time." He started up the ladder to the corridor. "Come on— we can get out where we came in. We can get the *Snooper* and go get dad at the Earth ship. And then we can get your father, and they'll *have* to listen to reason." He stopped suddenly, cocking his ear. "Listen! Do you hear something?"

David listened, and his face went white. The sound was clear now, a thin, high whistling noise, with a strange throbbing undertone. "That's a pump," David whispered. "We'd better hurry!"

They rushed upward, reaching the port completely out of breath. The whine was louder now, and the throbbing had become a clearly distinguishable pom-pom-pom of pumping pistons. They scanned the outside of the ship carefully, then slipped down the gangway, dousing their lights as they went. Once back in the tunnel they walked slowly, flicking their lights briefly every ten steps or so. "We'll have to dodge the Murexide," David whispered, "but it sounds like the pumps are nearby. That cave-in must have been *very* recent. It may have been the thing that was holding Cortell up all along."

"But how would they get to this side of the cave-in to set the pumps in motion?"

"They must have tunneled around the cave-in. It would have taken them two or three days, and that's about right—" He stopped short, and stepped gingerly

141

across the deadly gray strips in their path, then moved quickly along. They reached the Y, and still saw no one, but the sound of the pumps was imminent now. Carefully they crept along the wall, keeping the curve of the wall between them and the pumps—and then, almost on top of them, they heard voices, and froze against the wall—

"—still think there's something fishy about it," a voice was shouting above the pumps. "Don't have cave-ins like this just out of a clear blue sky. Especially when we're ready to get going—"

"Come on, get the bags in there and shut up," another voice snarled. "We got enough to do without crying about everything."

"Yeah, but why do they gotta make *us* do it?" There was a dull thump as another sandbag was slammed into place. "Who do they think we are, anyway? And it couldn't be a little break, nothin' like that. Oh, no. Gotta be four feet high—"

"All right, all right. Stop whining! Did you bring the sealer?"

There were more sounds, interspersed with grunts, and a hiss of the sealer pump as one of the men squirted the airtight plastic caulking over the sandbags. Tuck poked David, eyes wide with alarm. "They're closing up the opening!" he whispered hoarsely.

"I know it. Think I'm blind?"

"*But the Snooper!* It's outside! How'll we get back?"

David waved him to silence. One of the men was walking down the tunnel toward them. They shrank against the wall, hardly daring to breathe—

"*Now* where are you going, for the love of Mike?" The footsteps halted. "I thought I heard something—"

"Say, what are you afraid of—spooks?"

"Well, I don't like this. They might at least have given us guns—"

"Look, get back here and lend a hand, huh? Or maybe

142

you'd rather just sit and listen for bogeymen."

They heard the footsteps shuffle back again. Slowly David dropped to his belly, began slithering along the wall toward the voices. He moved very slowly, then suddenly motioned to Tuck. Tuck dropped too, and moved clumsily along the rough ground until he was very close. "Right behind you," he whispered.

"Good. The tunnel they dug through opens into this one about fifty feet from where they're working. They haven't got much light—if we move slow and quiet we might get past them. Careful!"

He started moving again, inching across the tunnel toward the black, raw hole that had been dug into the tunnel, around the cave-in. Tuck sneaked a look at the two burly workmen, toiling to get the sandbags thrown up to completely block the opening to the outside. Both were working in light, close-fitting pressure suits. They worked swiftly, grunting and cursing as they struggled with the bags. Tuck moved slowly, very slowly, desperately afraid some scratch, some joggled stone would rattle and betray them. But he suddenly saw David's feet disappear into the darkness of the tunnel, and with his heart racing, he eased himself up over the lip of the newly dug hole, slithered through, and lay panting, his heart pounding in his throat.

"Made it!" David was on his feet, crouched over in the narrow cut. "We'd better make speed."

"Where?"

"We can go back to the colony. There's probably a sealed entrance to this tunnel, coming off one of the main tunnels. If we can get into a main tunnel, we're all right—nobody can touch us. But if they catch us in here—" He solemnly drew his finger across the throat of the helmet. "Keep your fingers crossed."

They moved slowly, using their lights only when they needed to. "I don't think we need to worry about more Murexide," David whispered. "The stuff is too dangerous to mess around with, if they've had men moving supplies through here. Probably the one booby trap was considered protection enough." They hurried along as the tunnel started upgrading, winding slightly as they moved. Several times they passed through widened vaults, with cargo packed high against the walls; once they thought they heard steps ahead of them, and froze against the wall, only to realize that it was only rocks breaking loose from the roof and crunching down to the floor. Time passed, and still they walked, until Tuck began to doubt if they would ever reach the main tunnel. And then, like a flash, David dove for the floor. *"Down, Tuck!"*

Tuck fell like a poleaxed mule. He lay, face down, panting. Then he lifted his head, to confirm the glimpse of light that had struck his eyes a moment before.

There was no mistake. Ten feet ahead was a room, one of the widened vaults through which the tunnel passed. It had been dark, and then a light had suddenly gone on, almost in their faces. And in the room a man was pacing to and fro, his face lighted by the battle lamps in the vault, and he was talking in a loud, sharp, nasal voice that Tuck had heard once before, once too often.

The man was John Cortell.

Chapter 15

THE CLOSING BELL

THERE WAS no doubt of the man's identity. The thin, wiry frame, the pale hair, the narrow, hawk-like face— all were carved in Tuck's memory from his first sight of John Cortell. The man was angry now, and he paced the room like a caged wildcat, his voice sharp in the still air.

"I don't care if there were a thousand cave-ins, *we've got to get moving*, can't you see that? As long as we've got the colony to fight them off, we're doing fine, but how long do you think that can last?"

Another man's voice came to the boys from inside, a man they could not see. His voice was quiet, almost weary, and he was saying, "John, we've done everything we can. Cave-ins happen, and this one just came at the wrong time—"

"It sure did! It came so much at the wrong time that it smells from here to Earth and back!"

"John, you're getting nervous. You're dreaming things."

"Dreaning? With a cave-in in the one tunnel we have to have open?" The fugitive's voice rose desperately. "I don't like it. I've got a right to be nervous—"

"But nobody knows about it—they couldn't, or you'd have that Earth snooper and his whole crew in here on our necks right now. Relax, John. It'll just be a few more hours."

"And that idiot Farnham!" Cortell snarled. "Had to worry about Security catching up with him back on Earth—had to try to rub Benedict before he even left

Earth—" He ran a nervous hand through his pale hair. "Too much has gone wrong. We could have left *two days ago!* We could be gone, and the whole lousy crowd of them would be finished, and there wouldn't be a soul left to give Security a hint—"

Tuck listened, his confusion growing. He slowly edged his way back into the darkness, found David crouched close to the wall, listening. "Did you hear that? What's he talking about?" he whispered.

He heard David's breath, harsh in the darkness. "I don't quite know. Listen."

"But what is this place?"

"Looks like Cortell's main hide-out. It makes sense. He knows dad couldn't come for him here without giving away the whole works to the Colonel. And it's handy for making the ship ready. Cortell's no fool."

"But what can we do? We can't get through there into the colony—"

"That's for sure. And we can't go back." David's voice was edged with worry. "But they don't know we're here —and they don't know we're listening. And I want to hear the rest of this—"

They moved in closer to the opening. Tuck's mind was whirling, the thought screaming in his ears: your luck has run out, you're caught here, trapped! He tried to force the thought out, but it wouldn't force. They *were* caught—what if they hadn't been discovered yet? It was only a matter of time until somebody came back through the tunnel. Tuck glanced nervously over his shoulder into the blackness, straining to hear some sound of footfalls. He tried to think what they could do if the workmen were to suddenly come back down the tunnel, and he found to his horror that he couldn't even organize his thoughts—

"But we'll have to move fast when the time comes, because if Torm and the others even get a hint of it beforehand, it'll all be over." Cortell's voice was quieter now, but he still was pacing the narrow room. "We can't take any chances on it. That's one reason I'd like to see Torm killed now—with him gone, and maybe Ned Miller, they'd be running around like blind men. But on the other hand, it will be nice to think of him dying back here in the blowup, along with all the others—"

Tuck's eyes widened in horror. He glanced back at David, caught a glimpse of his face in the dim light, and repressed a shudder, turning back to listen again.

"I'm not sure I like that so much, either, John," the other man was saying. "The ship is outfitted for everyone. There's enough—"

"Garbage!" Cortell burst out. "It would take another ten years to outfit it for five hundred people." His voice lowered, almost confidentially. "Look, Dan, be reasonable. The supplies on that ship right now wouldn't keep five hundred people alive for fifty years—not a chance in a million, not even if everyone would take cut rations and co-operate a hundred percent. And that's the kicker—everyone won't. With five hundred people on that ship, there'd be murder and violence every step of the way. With five hundred people aboard, it wouldn't stand the breath of a chance." He stared at his companion, an ugly grin on his face. "But for *ten people*—five men and five women—there'd be plenty of supplies, plenty of food, plenty of water—and enough for the children when they come." Cortell sat down, nervously. "It's the only smart way to do it."

"I still don't like it."

"Look—there's me, and you, and Johnny Taggart, and Pete Yeakel and Rog Strang. And then there's our wives. Just the ten of us, on that ship, headed out. And not a trace left behind us, no mines, no colony, no Torm, no nothing—just one big, smoking crater to teach the Earth swine who they were meddling with—"

The other man was silent for a long time. Then he said, "The women won't like it, John. The men, sure, but the women—you know how they feel about—well, about the colony, about all the children—"

Cortell grinned nastily. "Now isn't that just too bad. It makes my heart ache, it does." His eyes were suddenly savage. "I've waited too long, Dan. If the women don't like it, that's tough. They come anyway. If they don't want to come, we drag them. But we've got to *move—*"

Tuck heard a swift movement at his elbow, a low-throated growl of rage. He caught David's arm violently, jerked it back, wrenching him sharply back. "Don't be a fool," he whispered. "Come on, we've got to get out of here—"

"I'll break his dirty neck," David snarled. "Let go of me, I tell you, I'll smash his skull in—

Tuck pinned the huge lad's arm back, suddenly savage himself. "Quiet! You'd wreck everything. Come on now!" His whisper was a sharp command in the darkness. David suddenly relaxed, stumbling along behind him, tears of fury rolling down his cheeks. "He's selling out everybody, the whole colony—"

"Well, you can't stop him that way." They crouched against the wall, well out of earshot of the hide-out. "Now listen. We've *got* to get back to the colony somehow, and fast. We can't do a thing by ourselves now. But we know where the ship is, and we know where Cortell is. We can lead your father to him, if we can stall Cortell, somehow. Now here's what I was thinking—"

Swiftly Tuck outlined the plan that had formed in his mind as he had listened to the men in the hideout. David listened intently, nodding every now and then. Then he said, "It might work—if the workers don't get us. And if we can stall him long enough—" They stood up, and started down the tunnel again, moving cautiously. The noise of their footfalls seemed deafening—surely they must be heard, back in the hide-out—but as they paused from time to time, straining to listen, they heard nothing but the sound of their own strained breathing. Occasionally they stopped to catch their breath, then forced on again. It seemed that they walked for miles, and then, far up ahead, they saw the workmen's lights, and slowed down to a cautious approach. "Do you think they'll be finished with the repair yet?"

David shook his head. "Can't tell. Maybe. But they'll have to pump out methane for another six hours before they dare let oxygen in."

"Maybe they won't try to let oxygen in. Why should they bother, if only ten people are coming through? They can certainly find ten pressure suits—"

David bit his lip, slowing to a stop. "Hadn't thought of that. But maybe we can fix them anyway." His eyes gleamed malignantly in the dim helmet light, and he searched around the floor of the tunnel until he found a couple of large rocks. "I think I can really fix things for them."

They could hear the pumps now, but there was no sign of activity at the other end of the newly dug tunnel. Slowly the boys inched forward, and Tuck stuck his head through the narrow opening, took a quick look, and drew it back sharply.

"One of them is right on the other side," he whispered. "But he's alone—"

"Think you can take him?"

Tuck nodded. "A lead pipe cinch, if he hasn't gotten a gun from the ship. They had quite an arsenal there, remember—homemade jobs, but deadly."

"Did you see him with a gun?"

Tuck shook his head. "Well, here goes," he whispered. With a crash he lunged through the opening into the tunnel, bringing an avalanche of rock and dirt down with him as he went. He got his balance in the tunnel just as the workman straightened up, alarm written a yard wide across his face. Before he could make a sound, Tuck was upon him, ripping out the talker-wires with a well-aimed swipe of his hand. The workman's curse was muffled as he tried to break from Tuck's grip, and with a powerful heave he threw Tuck down on his back on the tunnel floor. Like a cat the man was upon him, gripping his neck, lifting his head helmet and smashing it down on the floor. Tuck gave a wrench, and wriggled from his grasp, throwing the man off balance; then suddenly David's helmeted figure appeared from the open tunnel mouth, and caught the worker in a powerful half nelson. Two quick blows from David's heavy fist doubled him up on the ground, alive but quite helpless.

"Dirty fighting," grinned David as they started up the tunnel for the ship.

"Dirty guys," Tuck snapped back. "Better watch the talking now. I don't know where the other man is." They approached the Murexide strips gingerly, and as they crossed, Tuck noticed that David still carried the rocks. "What are those for?"

"You just watch," said David. They reached the opening into the crevice where the ship was. It was still quite dark and gloomy, but they could see the second workman up on the ramp near the Rocket Port, sitting on a box, busy scraping plastic sealer from his huge paws. He was completely oblivious to anything but his own troubles.

The boys flattened themselves in the shadow of the wall, slowly edging out of the tunnel mouth. Still the guard did not look up. Tuck moved along the wall, getting farther and farther from the tunnel mouth before he realized that David was still there. And then he saw David raise one of the rocks and heave it carefully into the tunnel; it struck the ground and rolled, and the guard looked up in alarm—

And then there was an earsplitting roar, shaking the ground like an earthquake, reverberating down the tunnel, and billows of dense, acrid Murexice smoke rolled out into the crevice. The guard ran down the ramp, and met a full body block from David, coming out of the smoke. The guard rolled over and over on the edge of the crevice as Tuck and David raced for the ramp. It was a short jump from the ramp to the nearest section of scaffolding, and then the boys were climbing like monkeys, higher and higher toward the rocky ledge at the top of the crevice. "Get the ship between us and the guard." Tuck roared, and they climbed even more frantically.

On the tunnel ledge below the guard was on his feet again, finally realizing that he'd been duped. There was a sharp crack, and Tuck heard a bullet whiz by his ear, followed by another, and another, both of which drove into and through the thin hull plating of the ship. Tuck scrambled as nimbly as he could, trying to get behind the ship, but the guard followed on the ledge below, trying to aim the gun with clumsy fingers on the trigger. A modern high-speed pellet gun would have succeeded, but this was an old-fashioned, home-forged revolver, clumsy and inaccurate. The bullets whizzed uncomfortably close, and then suddenly the guard was climbing after them, shouting hoarsely. David made a jump for the upper ledge, caught it and held, dragging himself up by brute strength. Then he leaned over and caught Tuck's wrist, and in an instant they were standing on top, with just a thin layer of plastic sealer between them and the outside.

David whipped out a knife, and started slashing the stuff, like putty. There was a hiss of inrushing gas as the methane broke through the airtight seal. Then David got his hand into the hole, and gave the stuff a powerful rip; it clung to his fist and tore like gum rubber, but the hole widened. The boys crawled through, then started ripping the sealer away as fast as they could. In a moment almost all of the camouflage was gone, leaving the formerly sealed-in crevice wide open, with the nose of the ship gleaming up at the purple sky.

And then they were running across the rocks, making for the *Snooper;* after a few minutes' climbing, they could see the little jet where they left it, gleaming in the fading sunlight, and they realized, almost with a shock, that they had been in the tunnel almost the whole Titan day. The guard finally reached the top of the scaffolding, and was shooting again, but the boys clambered into the cockpit of the little ship, and the motor was warmed before the guard got fifty feet. With a burst of blue flame the ship shot forward, and Tuck leaned back, his heart pounding in his throat as he felt the *Snooper's* nose rise into the sky.

A few moments later they were landing outside the air lock of the colony bubble, just as the lights were going on for the Titan night.

The night, Tuck reflected grimly, which bid fair to be the colony's last.

Chapter 16

"I'LL BACK YOU TO A MAN!"

ANSON TORM paced back and forth in the little stone cabin, his gray head bent, hands gripped tightly behind his back. He was alone—he had been alone for over an hour, listening to the minutes tick by, steadily, certainly. On the table lay a pile of papers; he stopped and leafed through them wearily. His fingers trembled on the type-written sheets, and he thought, here it is—the last duty in a lifetime of work. Here is the dotted line, Anson, for you to sign your colony's death warrant. Cortell has won, in the end, and you have lost, but it is you who must check the supply lists, it is you who must make sure that all the supplies are stored, all final details completed. Not far away, a ship stands waiting to carry your people to limbo, and soon they will wait no longer; soon they will file aboard—

The old man stared bitterly at the table top. He wanted to smash his fist down and roar with anger and frustration. If only they would think! If only he could make them understand what they were doing—And yet he knew it would do no good. This was the end of the line. The colonists would no longer support him, they believed Cortell when he told them that the time for revolt had come. And perhaps it had. Even his closest friend, Ned Miller, who fought at his side all these stormy years of leading the colony, had said, "There's nothing more we can do, Anson. If we oppose him now, Cortell will only kill us, and carry out the plan any-way—"

"But there must be some other way!"

153

"I don't know what. We knew it would come some-day. You knew it, and I knew it."

And Torm had spread his hands helplessly, and sank down in the chair, a tired, beaten old man. "But it need never have come," he said wearily. "It's so senseless, so hopeless—"

It was true. He knew in his heart that it was hopeless. The Colonel from Earth had dealt the last blow with his ultimatum, even as Cortell's men had moved through the colony, spreading hatred, whispering rebellion, arousing the colonists to fury. And now the end had come—there was no answer, no other way.

He sank down to the table, taking the first supply list from the pile with a heavy heart. And then the door burst open, and David was in the room, followed by the son of the Earth Colonel. Anson looked up, startled by the air of excitement that swept in the door with the boys; he saw their eyes go to the check lists on the table, and back to his face, and he felt a pang of shame. "Dad —you've got to come—"

Torm's eyebrows went up. "Come? Where?"

"To the Earth ship—now. Please, Dad, there's no time to waste!" There was an urgency in his son's voice, a frantic urgency Anson had never heard before. It struck a chord of hope in Anson's mind, but he shook his head wearily. "There's nothing we can gain at the Earth ship, son. There's no hope there or anywhere."

"Dad, *we've found the star-ship—*"

Anson Torm lurched to his feet as if he had been struck. "That's enough, David!" he snapped. "What kind of nonsense—"

David Torm shook his head, glancing at Tuck. "He already knows, Dad, there's no reason to be quiet. We were together, we couldn't have done it by ourselves, neither of us. We found the ship, and we know where Cortell is hiding."

Torm's face was gray. "David, David—"

"Dad. we've got to see Colonel Benedict. We found

154

Cortell's hide-out, we heard what he was saying—" Swiftly he told his father what they had heard, Cortell's plan of treachery. The Colony leader's face grew darker as he listened; he began trembling so violently he could hardly control his hands. "There's no mistake, David? You couldn't have been wrong?"

"There was no mistake, believe me—"

And then Torm was on his feet, struggling into a pressure suit, his eyes haunted. "We'll have to get to the Earth ship," he said. "We can get a half-track—"

"There's not enough time for that. The *Snooper* will carry us, if we're lucky."

Approximately five minutes later the little jet plane was swooping up into the purple sky away from the colony, leaving a trail of snow in its wake, heading like a carefully aimed arrow for the rocket ship from Earth at the Rocket Landing—

Cortell had been sleeping when the guard burst into the hide-out from the ship tunnel, panting, clutching his side, dragging a leg after him as he walked. He staggered to a seat, gasping. "They ripped open the ship's camouflage," he choked, "broke the whole thing open, and they got away. I couldn't stop them—"

Cortell had the man by the throat, shaking him savagely. "Who? How did they find it? *Who was it?*"

"Torm's boy, and someone else, I don't know who. They jumped us—I don't know how they found us, I don't know where they came from. They blew up the Murexide and tried to cave in the tunnel, but the beams held—"

Cortell was on his feet, trembling like a wildman when Dan Carver returned. "Get the men," he snarled. "Get them, and get their women. The word will be out any minute—" He pointed silently to the guard.

Dan's jaw sagged, and his face went white. "I just saw Pete and Rog headed this way—"

"Well, *get the others!*" Cortell screamed. "There's no time—"

"But the leak—"

"Let it leak, let it leak forever. We'll use the supplies we've got, go aboard in suits. But we've got to go—" There was fear in his face now, fear that almost over-shadowed the cunning, and as Dan started back for the colony, Cortell began packing a supply bag furiously, his eyes darting toward the tunnel, with the fear widening every minute—

Because he knew, coldly, that he was fighting against time now, and time was running out.

Colonel Benedict's face was white as the two boys and Anson Torm filed into the cabin. He didn't look at Tuck, but there was anger in his eyes, and a hurt that was more painful to Tuck than any anger could have been. He stared at them, and when he found his voice, he said, "Did you bring Cortell with you?"

And then the boys were talking, one after another, telling everything. So very much had happened that they could hardly contain themselves. They told him the whole story, and then of their stumbling upon Cortell's hiding place, and of the treachery they had heard as they waited, shivering, in the black tunnel outside.

And when they were finished, the anger was gone from the Colonel's eyes, the hurt was vanished. Instead, he looked stunned, shaken beyond belief. He sat down at the desk and stared at them as though they were ghosts, and twice when he tried to speak, words failed him. And then, finally, his voice was very low. "You found this—the two of you, together? David? Tuck?"

The boys nodded.

"It's incredible. Utterly incredible."

Anson Torm's blue eyes caught the Colonel's, held them bravely. "It's true. Every word of it."

"You're telling me that this colony of men and women

156

have been working in secret *for over a century*—to build this ship?"

"I'm telling you that."

"At the risk of being caught at any time?"

Torm nodded. "They recognized that risk."

The Colonel shook his head numbly. "But there is no interstellar drive."

"Desperation and courage would be their interstellar drive."

"It would take them centuries! They could never return—"

"It would be better than to stay here as slaves."

"But not even knowing that they would find anything when they got there—"

"It would still be better." Anson Torm's voice trembled. "I fought against it—oh, how I fought against it. But I had to guard the secret, too. I couldn't tell you about it. I dared not tell you."

The Colonel shook his head like a man in a dream. "It's incredible. And yet, it's in the human tradition—to go to any length, if a chance of freedom lies at the end—"

He walked slowly across the room. Then he turned to Anson Torm, his eyes on the leader's careworn face. "You colonists must be proud and brave men," he said. He glanced at the boys, his eyes suddenly proud. "We've been fools—both of us. It's taken them to show us what fools, but I'm beginning to see things now that I'd never have believed." He looked up gravely at Anson Torm. "I—I just don't know what to say. I've been so hidebound and devoted to authority that I've let it blind me. I'm truly sorry. Perhaps there's still time to salvage something." He held out his hand to the colony leader. "I'll back you to a man, Anson. I'll back this colony in every way I can. We'll have to stop Cortell, if the boys can lead us to him, and try to break his plan right now. And then I think there'll be some changes for the Titan colony. I don't know how I can do it—I'm only one man; they may never believe me, but I'll fight for all I'm worth. I'll open their eyes, somehow, I'll get your story before the legislative bodies back on Earth, get it to the ears where it will do some good. And there will be some changes made, if it's the last thing I do. This time, Earth won't let you down."

Ten minutes later the four of them were bent excitedly over a huge map of the underground mining tunnel and a topographical map of the region which David had made. "This is the place where the entrance to the ship tunnel is," Torm was saying. "It's carefully concealed where it breaks from this main tunnel, and Cortell will have it guarded. And this—" he pointed beyond the area marked *radioactives*, "is the location of the ship."

The Colonel studied the picture. "We should approach from both ends, in case they move faster than we anticipate," he said. "You know the colony, Anson. Suppose you take David, get as many men as you can, and go in from the colony side. We're closer to the ship right here, so Tuck and I can take the men from here and go in at that end." He looked up, and Torm nodded approval. "And we want to take him alive, if we can," the Colonel added. "We've got to get the support of the colony behind you again, and for good."

David and his father left in the *Snooper*. The Colonel and Tuck and four crewmen from the Earth ship clambered into the half-track that stood on the ground below, and plunged up the rim of rocks along the route David had charted for them. The trip took almost an hour; Tuck sat forward, watching the compass, directing the driver of the 'track from time to time. He hardly dared to breathe as he peered ahead for the first sign of the ruined camouflage, seeking the bright glint of the starship's pointed nose rising above the rocks. A thousand fears crept slyly through his mind—what if the ship had been sealed up already, so that they would have to stumble over it to find it? The cave-in would still be there, but even that would be invisible until they stumbled upon it. And what if Cortell changed his plans, tried a break with the ship before they arrived to stop him? The minutes passed, and tension mounted; then suddenly Tuck let out a shout, and pointed beyond the next ridge of rocks.

And they saw it—the pointed nose of the ship, gleaming in the sunlight, sticking up from the protecting rim of the crevice. The half-track moved cautiously, approaching within thirty yards of the crevice. Then the Colonel signaled to the driver to stop. "Better go on foot," he said. "We're sitting ducks in this thing."

They clambered out of the vehicle—the four men from the crew armed with projectile guns, the Colonel with his own service automatic gripped in his suited hand. Tuck carried a small Barnet shocker, his finger curled against the release stud. Slowly the men fanned out, moving toward the crevice, their boots clanking on the rocks as they advanced over the coarse terrain—

A shot rang out, and one of the men clutched his side, toppled forward on the rocks. "Cover!" the Colonel snapped, and they dived for the rocks as shots began raining on them from the ship. There were two men there, armed with the homemade automatics that Tuck had seen before, but these men were more deadly in their aim. The bullets whizzed by Tuck's ears, striking the rocks around him as the men slowly slid forward toward the ship. Then the Colonel eased around a rock, let go four quick shots, and they heard one of the men groan and crash to the ground. Like a flash, two of the crewmen raced forward ten feet through a hail of fire, then dropped again, panting. A thought occurred to Tuck; he started for an outcropping of rock to the right as another volley of shots came from the ship. The gunman's attention was held by the crewmen sneaking up on him, and he was too well-concealed for them to get in a shot. Tuck quickly moved into flank the ship, then clambered slowly up on the high, jagged ridge that overhung the crevice. Far below he saw the glint of sunlight on a pressure helmet, and with all his strength he ripped off a huge chunk of rock, and hurled it downward—

The rock struck the helmet a crashing blow, and the man reeled, firing savagely up toward Tuck. Too late he realized that he had revealed himself; the Colonel's gun chattered sharply, and the gunman gripped his side, trying to scramble back. For a long second he teetered; then his footing slipped, and he fell crashing into the crevice, down between the ship's wall and the protecting rock, and struck with a sickening thud at the bottom—

The three crewmen and the Colonel met Tuck at the edge of the crevice. One of the crewmen was dispatched to care for the man who had been hit; the rest of them jumped for the ship's scaffolding, and began to clamber down like monkeys. In a moment they were moving down the tunnel, over the rocks and debris that had been torn down by the Murexide explosion, and then into the blackness that led to Cortell's hide-out.

For a long while there was silence, broken only by the plodding of their feet, echoing and re-echoing weirdly from the rocky walls of the tunnel. Then up ahead they heard shots and shouts. At a signal from the Colonel they stopped, then moved forward cautiously. Quite suddenly, they saw a bobbing light up ahead, then another. The Colonel hissed, and they crouched along the walls, their own lights out, and waited, panting, as the frantic footfalls came closer. And then two figures materialized behind the bobbing lights; one of the crewmen pounced on the first man, and the lights went crashing to the ground. The second man made a break, tripped on an outstretched leg, and tumbled down, skidding on the ground. The tunnel exploded into a crashing uproar of scuffling and curses; then, like a knife, a bright light snapped on, a battle lamp one of the men had carried, and they saw their prizes, panting, caught like rats in a trap.

Dan Carver was whimpering, his face a mask of fear

160

as he peered up at his captors. "Don't tell them," he was babbling, "Don't tell them—take us back to Earth, do anything, but don't let them know—" He collapsed into frightened tears, sobbing like a baby. But John Cortell just stared around him as though he didn't believe what he saw, and then sank to the ground, a snarl on his lips. "If you want me back in the colony," he rasped, "you'll carry me—"

The Colonel stared down in contempt at the traitor, then jerked a thumb at him, and nodded to two of the crewmen. "Carry him," the Colonel said.

Chapter 17

A FEARFUL CHOICE

THE AIR was heavy with bloodshed. It hung in the huge underground meeting hall of the Titan colony; it echoed from the dark walls, and dripped from the dead rock carved generations before; it hung on every face, every grim-faced man and woman in the hall. Bloodshed hovered in the room like a ghost as the men and women gathered, muttering to each other in low tones. The faces were bitter faces, with their violence barely repressed; the mutterings were the noises of an angry crowd, driven to its limit, and when Colonel Benedict and Anson Torm walked down the center aisle to the front of the room, muttering rumbled at their heels like a gathering storm. Their eyes were turned toward Torm and the Colonel, sullen eyes that carried the savage gleam of desperation and hatred.

And then the guards entered with John Cortell—a surly faced Cortell, face red with anger, eyes that carried an underlying image of fear. The colonists saw him, half-dragged to the front of the room, and the angry muttering broke into an uproar that drowned words in a fever of cries and gestures. Fists were shaken in Anson Torm's face. A voice cried out, "Let him go!" and a hundred shouts of approval rose like a tide in the tension-laden room.

Then Anson Torm stood up, his face grim, sweat standing out on his forehead as he faced the angry crowd. "I want every man and woman in the colony down here," he shouted above the tumult. "Is everybody here?"

Somebody shouted, "Everybody's here—get on with it!"

"Then let's have it quiet!" The uproar stilled slightly, as all eyes turned to Torm's face. "The Colonel from Security told us to have Cortell in his hands by sundown," Torm cried. "All right. Cortell is in his hands, as directed." He turned cold eyes to Cortell's face as a pandemonium of protest broke loose from the crowd. "Let's have it quiet!" he cried again. "Cortell has some things to tell you—before he's turned over to Earth courts on charges of treason!"

The uproar burst out again, angrily. A man jumped up in the back of the room, shaking his fist in the air. "Anson Torm is the only traitor in this room—"

A cheer went up, and for an instant it looked as if the colonists would rise up and mob the colony leader. The crewmen around Cortell turned to face the crowd, guns raised defensively. And then, like a cat, Cortell caught the nearest guard a brutal blow to the side of the neck, wrenched his gun from his hand as he fell. Cortell jumped up on a chair, gun raised above his head, and a cheer went up from the crowd as the gun lowered straight for Colonel Benedict's head. *"One move, and the Earth spy will be dead!"* Cortell shouted above the uproar.

A hush fell on the room, a sudden, breathless stillness. The sullenness died on the colonists' faces, and a cheer went up. "You tell 'em, John! You tell 'em who the traitor is!"

Cortell's voice was an angry rasp as his eyes shot around to one of the Earth ship's crewmen who was moving slowly back behind him. *"Not a move!* I warn you! Even if you could shoot me, your precious Colonel would never escape this room. And as for our fine colony leader—" He turned his eyes to Torm, jubilantly. "The shoe is on the other foot now, and you'd better not forget it. You're through with your yellow-bellied deals and your lies, Torm—as of now!"

The room was full of cheers now. Some of the men were on their feet, ready to move forward at a glance from Cortell. But others hesitated, and waited—

And then, very slowly, Anson Torm walked to the table, and leaped up on top of it, high above the group, so that every man in the room could see him. "He's a very brave man with a gun—yes, a very brave man." Torm's eyes flashed about the room. "Well, I have no gun. Take a look—my hands are empty. But I've got something to say, and you're going to listen—"

"Nobody wants to hear you," somebody snarled, and there were cheers and threatening fists. Cortell's face darkened with anger; he started to speak, and then caught Torm's eye. And something held him. He sneered, and stuck his hand in his pocket as Anson Torm started to speak.

"Cortell talks about yellow deals—well, listen to the deal I've made. We've won our fight—do you hear that? The Colonel came here as an enemy of all of us—he's sitting here now as a friend. We've asked for equality—he'll fight to give us equality. We've fought for representation, for education, for the right to go back to Earth as men, to be regarded as men—all right, he'll fight to give us those rights." Torm's voice rose sharply. "We've fought against the lies and propaganda that have reduced us to the level of slaves—he'll stop that propaganda, and tell the truth about Titan to the ends of the Earth! The Colonel has pledged us these things, and he'll keep his promises."

A mutter went up from the crowd, but Torm cut them off sharply. "But Cortell here has told you that these things will never happen. No Earthman can be trusted, he says, the time for rebellion has come, the best solution to our problems is to go aboard the ship which waits for us, leave Titan, leave our homes, leave the Solar System, take what providence will offer us and our great-great-grandchildren who remain at the end of such a voyage. This is what Cortell has been telling you, isn't it? It wouldn't be suicide, he says, there would be freedom for all of us, he says—isn't that what he says?" Torm's eyes turned to Cortell, bitterly. Cortell's face had gone dead white, and a smile appeared on Torm's lips. "How about that, John? Did you mean freedom for everybody? Or for just a few of your friends? Tell them about your plan, John! Tell them how you figured that the fewer people who embarked on the journey, the greater the chances for success. Tell them why you planned to leave secretly, to gather your four close friends and their wives together and leave. Why don't you speak up, John? Why don't you tell them how you planned to blast off with the ship and leave them here to die when you ignited the mines—"

There was bewilderment on the faces of the crowd now, and disbelief. Eyes were wide, turned to John Cortell. They turned, and saw Cortell's face, a white, frightened mask, and realization began to dawn—

"It's a lie!" Cortell screamed. "Don't listen to him! He's afraid, he's cornered, and he knows it, and he's lying—"

"Well, who are you going to believe?" Torm cried to the colonists. He pointed an accusing finger at Cortell. "Look at him! And then look at me. Think back, and try to remember the last time I've lied to you in the last thirty years—think! Cortell says I'm afraid—well, *look at him*, and then look at me, and see who's afraid—and then remember how many times you've seen me afraid—" Torm's eyes were blazing now, and his head was high. "Count the times you've seen me cower and cringe and go white with fear—go ahead, name the times! Name the times you've seen me a coward. Count the lies you've heard from my lips—and then *look at the man who accuses me!*

The faces were turned to John Cortell now, white faces, faces with the truth dawning in them. A hundred faces turned to him, two hundred, and voices began to rise. "Listen!" Torm cried. "I told you he's betrayed you—that he planned to leave in secret with Carver and Taggart and Strang and Yeakel, to take your ship and leave you behind. He was all ready to go when we caught him—" He glanced narrowly at the rear of the room, and said, "Well, we can prove it! Look around you! *Who is missing from the room right now?*"

Eyes looked around, wide, frightened eyes, eyes filling with sudden suspicion. There was a hush over the room; then a woman let out a gasp and cried, "Their wives! *Where are their wives?*"

There was silence, as though a huge curtain had fallen over the room. Then Torm said, "Bring 'em in, Ned. Show the people who we found on board the star-ship!"

There was a scuffle on the stairs, and then four figures were pushed down the center aisle, figures still clad in pressure suits. The room was still as death as they marched forward—Dan Carver's wife, Johnny Taggart's wife, Rog Strang's wife, John Cortell's wife. They moved forward like people condemned, their hands covering their faces—

And then, as the crowd rose in fury, Cortell jumped down from the chair with a roar, gun tight in his fist. Slowly he backed toward the stairs, covered on either side by Pete Yeakel and Rog Strang. His face was a mask of fear now, and when he reached the stairs he broke and ran as the mob fell upon his lieutenants. One of the Earth ship's crewmen was up the stairs in a flash, jerking his gun from its holster as he ran. Cortell was heading for the main tunnels; his footfalls rang out on the cold rock ground, until a shot rang out, and he fell, arms flung out, and lay kicking helplessly, blood streaming from his leg. And then the crewmen were around him, keeping back the colonists, waving down the bitter shouts, until stretcher-bearers came from the infirmary, and Doc Taber took over, and Cortell was taken away. And then they turned again, and went back to the hall.

It was much later when Ned Miller appeared at the

door to Anson Torm's cabin, just as the Colonel and Tuck were finishing supper. He stood in the doorway, awkwardly, rubbing his stubbled chin, twisting his mining cap in his hands. Then finally he stepped inside, nodded uncomfortably at the Earth Colonel.

"You did a fine job, Ned," Anson Torm said. "The timing was perfect—and I thought you'd find the women aboard the ship, especially when I couldn't spot a one of them in the crowd—"

Ned nodded uneasily. "Anson," he said, "I've got to say something—"

Torm looked up, "What is it, Ned?"

The little miner shifted from one foot to the other. "I've been neglected," he blurted finally. "Some of the men got together, after the meeting was over. They want me to talk for them—" He looked up, his eyes unreadable.

Torm stood up in alarm. "What's the trouble?"

"We want to go," said Ned Miller softly. "We want to take the ship and go—"

Torm's jaw sagged. "Ned! What are you saying?"

"We mean it, Anson. The Colonel's given us promises —I know that. But we've heard promises from Earthmen before. Many promises, wonderful promises. And always, in the end, we were worse off than before—"

"Ned, this is different now!"

"I know you believe that," the little man said doggedly. "We—we'd like to. But we can't."

Torm's face was white. "What are you trying to say, Ned?"

"I'm saying we've worked on the ship for years. I've worked on it, without knowing what I was working on —until today. But I knew it was a hope against hope, something we could count on, something we could build our faith into. There's nothing here for me. not any more, not that my faith built into that ship. And there are a lot of men who feel the same way. They're afraid the Earthman will go aboard his ship tomorrow and take it up, and bomb our star-ship to smithereens. And then where would our hope be? Then what would prevent him from coming back down, and throwing us all into chains—even you? Or if not this Earthman, then the next, or the next after him. It would be the end, the bitter end of four generations of work—"

Torm sat silent for a long time. Then he said, "What do your men want to do, Ned?"

"There are a hundred and forty of us—men, women and children. We talked, and we all feel the same. We want to take the ship and go."

Torm's face was gray. "You know the chances of ever finding a landing—"

"We know. But it's a hope. We can have faith in it. The star-ship is the only answer, for us. If the others want to stay, take their chances, that's their choice. For us, we want to take the ship while we can."

Torm looked at him, the weariness of long years written on his face. "I—I can't give you permission, Ned. That's the man who can give you permission, or not, as he sees fit." He looked sadly at Colonel Benedict.

Ned turned to the Colonel, a desperate light in his eyes. "If you mean the promises you've made to Anson, then prove your faith. Give us permission to go."

Colonel Benedict stared at the man. "Why, to allow you to take that ship would be to violate every principle of the Earth Security Commission. I'd be liable to a a strange light in his eyes. "It would be the biggest general court-martial. It's unthinkable—" he stood up, "scandal Security has had on its hands for a hundred years—Anson, do you realize what it could mean? It would bring a wholesale, total investigation of the whole Earth-Titan relationship!" He stared at the colony leader, excitedly. "It would bring this colony under the spotlight like never before. People could *see* what's been happening out here; they could see the truth about the colony, instead of the lies they've been hearing! Why, Security would be turned inside out with investigation, and in a court-martial I could tell the truth, and there would be no brushing my report aside—they'd *have* to listen!"

"Then you'll let us go?" Ned Miller's voice was eager.

"Let you? You have my full, official permission—I'll give it to you in writing, with an Earth Security seal!"

Ned turned to Anson Torm. "We have Security's permission, Anson," he said. "We want our leader's permission."

Torm sighed. "Make me a listing of passengers," he said. "We'll help you finish supplying the ship and make it ready. And as for us who remain—" He looked proudly at Colonel Benedict. "We've got a fight on our hands. The sooner we make our plans, the better—"

Chapter 18

"WHEN TWO STRONG MEN—"

THE NEXT days were exhausting. The list of the colonists who were leaving on the star-ship was long; the men studied it carefully, and the weariness grew in Anson Torm's eyes as he checked name after name—friends of many years, men and women he had known and loved and fought for. Yet he knew that for them, their decision was the right one. The years of hatred and bitterness had left its mark on the colony, a mark that nothing could erase, a mark so deep that no human decision could now change it. And behind that mark was the knowledge that a hundred years of work and sorrow lay behind their decision.

The boys pitched in with the rest in the tremendous task of making the ship ready for its final journey. With only a hundred and forty people aboard, the chances for a successful voyage were far greater than they ever could have been with the whole colony. But the boys saw something that their fathers perhaps did not see— they could see the greatness of the adventure, they could feel the call of the unknown challenge that lay before the ship. They worked in bright-eyed eagerness as they saw the supplies rolling up the ramp, the few personal belongings of the embarking colonists installed in the tiers of small lockers in the huge sleeping quarters of the ship. Here was the call of the stars—one small ship, manned by men who had no place in the land they were leaving. The ship sat still and proud as the work progressed, its silver nose pointed toward the dark sky, and as the boys worked, their excitement grew.

At dinners, and in the evenings, they could talk of nothing else. The Colonel and Anson Torm watched them, feeling the excitement stir in their own minds, even as they listened. But then, finally, the work was done, and the ship was ready. Torm and the Colonel had agreed to wait until then before settling down to the plans that lay ahead for the colony; there was too much work to be done, too much excitement to talk and think of anything else. But finally the night before the leave-taking arrived, and Torm walked out of the cabin and found Tuck Benedict and David sitting quietly in front of the cabin, watching the yellow rings of Saturn as it rode high in the sky, talking a little, but mostly sitting in silence, watching.

The old man sat down beside them. They hardly noticed him, so he sat and watched, too. And then, finally, he said, "It's a great adventure. We'll never know if they get to their destination, or when, or how many. We'll never live to know." He raised a finger, pointed to a tiny spot of brightness in the cloud of stars. "Those are the Centauris there—where they're heading. Even they will never know if those to come will get there, or whether they will find anything when they do."

The boys sat mutely watching, and Anson Torm's eyes were on his son's face as he stared up. There were so many things he wanted to say to his son, so many, many things—and yet he knew that he and David were a million miles apart, that he could never understand the longing that had been in his son since he had first toddled out of the cabin and pointed toward the bright stars, and said, "I want that, Daddy—" He saw David's broad shoulders, the unruly shock of blond hair, the brightness in his eyes. He sat looking at David for a long time. Then he said, "You can go with the ship if you want to, son. If that's where you belong—if you really believe that—I'll not try to stop you—" The old man's voice trembled.

David turned wide, wondering eyes to his father. "It's what I've always dreamed of—going there—"

"I know. That's why I'd never stop you."

Tuck watched the two, his heart suddenly beating wildly. He realized that David had taken the words from his mouth, stated in one short, simple sentence all the excitement and longing and adventure he felt in his own heart. David was silent for a long time. Then he said, "I should be the leader here, after you go—isn't that right, Dad?"

Anson Torm's eyes were grave. "Torms have been elected to lead the Titan colony for generations, son. Your father, your grandfather, his father before him . . . they've been good leaders."

"And there's work to be done—here at home. You and the Colonel will be able to make a start—but what about twenty years from now? Who will do the work then?" He looked at the stars again, and then his eyes caught his father's. "We've been talking, Tuck and I," he said softly. "We've been thinking about things a good bit lately—the whole history of the Titan colony, and what there is to look forward to here. And Tuck is going back to study, and help his father fight for the colony, back on Earth. Last night the Colonel told me that he had friends who would help me arrange to take admission exams for the Polytechnic Institute, if I wanted to—" He glanced at Tuck, then dropped his eyes. "I'm not going to do it. And I'm not going with the ship. I think I belong here—on Titan. With me here, and Tuck back on Earth—we'll finish what you two have started."

Anson Torm looked at the boys, first one, then the other, and his voice didn't seem to work right when he tried to speak. "That's your decision—the two of you?"

"The two of us. That's our decision. Oh, Tuck will come out here when he has a chance. We've got great plans, Dad—we want to see some of Saturn's moons that haven't been mapped yet, maybe even go in to Saturn herself, someday. And Japetus—we'll land there one of these days, Geigers or no Geigers. And I'll go back to Earth to visit, too. But that's just play, in the long run. The real work is here."

For a long moment Torm sat, staring at the stars, his heart crying things he could never find words to say. And then, finally, he rose and walked back to the cabin. At the door he paused, his face happier than David had seen it in years. "We'll be seeing the ship off in the morning," he said. "Better get some sleep."

It was early, with the light just rising above the horizon when the last man walked up the ramp, and turned to wave to the group gathered below, then closed the port behind him, slowly, until it locked with a final clang. The group walked away, walking back from the crevice where the ship stood. Far back there were sandbag barriers to protect the remaining colonists from the blast. The people found their places, and waited in the still Titan morning. There were many tears, and much sadness on many faces. They waited, and it seemed that the minutes that ticked by were an eternity long—and then they heard the rumble, a whining groan which rose to a roar, shaking the ground with its power.

A billow of powdery white rose around the silver nose of the star-ship, enveloping it in an iridescent cloud, and then slowly and majestically the nose of the ship began to rise through the cloud. The jets bellowed yellow flame, and the roar echoed and re-echoed down the gorges and canyons of the planet. The ship rose, higher and higher, faster and faster, like a silver arrow in the sky, leaving its streamer of white behind it. Slowly it turned, slowly it dwindled, and the roar faded away in their ears, asd with a last glint of silver the ship shrank to a tiny dot, blinked, and was lost from view.

The people were silent as they made their way back to the colony, silent with an emptiness that they could nei-

173

ther explain nor express. The boys walked side by side, saying nothing, and a few yards behind them, Colonel Benedict and Anson Torm walked, almost surprised that they needed no words to communicate their feelings. In a few moments they would be seated at a table, an Earthman and a colonist working in trust and confidence for the peace and prosperity, of both Earth and Titan, for the first time in generations. It would be a hard job —they both knew that. A court-martial might ruin the Colonel's career. But if it would bring the truth to the attention of Earth lawmakers, if it would expose the cruelty and tyranny of the Security Commission's policy toward Titan, it would be worth the fight. And both men knew in their hearts that it would succeed.

As they walked, Colonel Benedict smiled, and pointed ahead to David and Tuck. "Thick as thieves," he said quietly. "I wonder why they could see so much more clearly than we could? Two boys from the ends of the Solar System!"

"Boys?" said Anson Torm. "I wonder. They were boys a week ago, that's true. But they were talking like men last night." He smiled, his eyes misty. "There was an old Earth ballad my grandfather used to recite to me when I was young." His eyes rested on the boys as they walked along. "Kipling, I think:

"But there is neither East nor West, Border, nor Breed, nor Birth,
When two strong men stand face to face, though they come from the ends of the earth!"

The two men glanced at each other, then back to the boys. And the sun shone brightly on the Titan colony.